the Phantom Portrait

WHITE RAVEN SERIES BOOK 2

AnneMarie Dapp

THE PHANTOM PORTRAIT
Copyright © 2020 by AnneMarie Dapp

ISBN: 978-1-68046-999-8

Published by Satin Romance
An Imprint of Melange Books, LLC
White Bear Lake, MN 55110
www.satinromance.com

Published in the United States of America.

Cover Design by Ashley Redbird Designs

To Darci and Christina
Thank you for helping me solve the mysteries of life.

"But don't you see that I must go, for it seems that I am cut in half and only one part of me here. The other piece is over the sea, calling and calling me to come and be whole."

— JOHN STEINBECK

Prologue

JADE MACKENZIE WHISPERED A PRAYER FOR HER MOTHER.

She'd just finished her grad program in art history when her mother's illness had taken a sharp turn for the worse. She needed a fresh start. Somewhere peaceful, where she could begin to heal. The cool ocean breeze blew sandy blond locks around a heart-shaped face while tears fell from steel-gray eyes. She walked along the mossy trail, glancing over the grounds of the Queen of Heaven Cemetery. The woman watched as a seagull landed atop a marble statue of the Virgin Mary, squabbling up at the darkening sky. Turning her back, she hurried across the manicured lawn toward her vehicle while pressing the key fob. The door clicked open with a sharp beep and she climbed inside the chilly Ford pickup.

With her wipers on high, she drove down Highway 101 heading to Monterey. An icy wind sent goosebumps over her flesh, so she rolled up the windows and flipped on the heat. She passed miles of sand dunes and colorful ice plants, the waves crashing together along the beach, foamy peaks rising from the glassy currents. Sea lions stretched lazily along granite boulders, basking in the fleeting rays of the setting sun. Thunder boomed overhead, the afternoon sky darkening eerily over the valley.

Her mind drifted while she drove, shooting toward the glovebox, considering the new deed. Her mother had said she could use the family cottage while setting up her shop, but it still felt like she was trespassing.

She parked her truck behind the old, newly-hers cottage, grabbed her purse, the newly-inherited diary of her great-grandmother, and bag of groceries and then slipped down onto the sandy beach.

Seagulls cried, diving towards the raging waters. Jade stopped a moment, gazing at the shoreline, watching the garnet rays fading towards the horizon. She walked up the cobblestone path to the front of the modest cottage, briefly noticing the weather-worn exterior. She ran the tip of her finger over the coarse boards, peeling off a few flakes of paint in the process.

There was quite a lot of work to do fixing up the old place. She was almost ready to sign on a foreclosed space in Pacific Grove that held an antique shop that she wanted to remake and open, so at least the cottage was closer to the shop than her mother's house where she'd moved once it was clear her mother wasn't going to get better. Juggling a cottage renovation and new business seemed like a daunting task. Taking a deep breath, her hand reached toward the copper knob, and then her key clicked into place. She pushed the door open with a groan from its hinges. At the same moment, streaks of lightning flashed above as a white missile shot past her right side, landing by her feet in a blur of snowy feathers.

She gasped, reaching toward the injured bird fluttering on its side. The creature thrashed the ground, trying in vain to fly, the right wing bent at a startling angle. Pale eyes caught her gaze, and she knew in an instant what she must do. She scooped the bird up and made her way into the darkness.

The cottage was musty and in need of a good cleaning. Old books and vintage collectibles layered in thick dust were cluttered about the room. An empty wire basket sat in the corner by the hearth, so she placed it on the table, then pulled her scarf from her neck and lined the bottom. She held it before her to examine her new charge and its injury. It looked like a baby raven. But white. She wrapped the wing gently with a piece of linen from the sewing box. Satisfied with her doctoring, she placed the baby raven inside the basket. She studied the bird in astonishment, not quite sure what to make of it. The baby appeared healthy, other than the injured wing, but its feathers, which should have been ebony in color, were shockingly white. The fledgling nibbled the soft scarf, then fluffed its feathers and began to preen, eyes fixed on its new caretaker. Within a few minutes, the creature surrendered to sleep inside the makeshift nest. Jade looked at her charge with a soft smile, then moved toward the fireplace, starting the logs with a lighter and bit of old newspaper. She sighed as the room warmed and shadows receded to the far corners of the room.

Warm June rain pounded the tin roof as the wind rattled the windows in their vintage frames. She looked around, listening to the fire crackle in the hearth; *Everything was old, yet so familiar,* she thought.

Once she'd kicked off her shoes and put away the groceries, she opened a bottle of local Chardonnay and poured herself a generous glass. Outside, the storm raged, shaking the cottage to its foundations. Thunder boomed and lightning flashed behind lace curtains. Taking a seat at the edge of the bed, she reached for the gold-leaf diary. For the next several hours, she traveled back in time, enraptured by her ancestor's journey. Turning the final page released a pearly white feather which slipped from the binding. Jade held it up to the firelight in wonder, tears blurring her vision. Considering the snowy quill, she realized her own story was only beginning.

Chapter One

FOG DRIFTED IN SINISTER SHADOWS BEFORE HER EYES. SHE MOVED TOWARD THE sounds of the ocean, hands splayed out, searching for something just out of reach. The fluttering of wings echoed below. Crumbling soil rolled off the ledge, and she looked out at the snow-white ravens.

They flew toward the frigid waters, disappearing into the thick fog. A pod of seals rose from the dark currents. The largest of the group reached the cove and immediately began galumphing across the sand dunes. It paused, the rays of sun settling onto its slippery back. The sky darkened and lightening streaked over the horizon. With a low moan, the animal writhed and dug its flippers into the ground. A crimson line etched down its torso while the skin peeled back. She gasped as she listened to the creature's wails. Something was happening, something unbelievable. The young woman moved closer to the edge of the cliffside while the ground quaked beneath her feet. She fell, and then there was nothing...but darkness.

Jade sat bolt upright, reaching blindly in the dark. Her hand settled over the vibrating cell phone and she pulled it to her ear.

"Hello?"

A stranger's voice was on the other end.

"Is this Jade Mackenzie?"

"Yes. Who's this?"

"This is a courtesy call from Bay Alarm. There's been a reported incident at 1222 Lighthouse Avenue."

She absently rubbed her eyes while her heart raced. Sitting up in bed, she rolled her legs over the side.

"Oh, god. That's my shop. Was there a break in?"

"Can't say for sure. The smoke detector was triggered, and the fire department is on their way."

The young woman sucked in her breath, blinking in the darkness. "I'll be right over. Thank you."

Trembling on the cold hardwood floor, she flicked on the Tiffany lamp by the bedside. Half awake, she made her way to her closet and slipped into a pair of sweats and hoodie, then fumbled for her Keds at the bottom of the closet.

Her hands shook as she twisted her sandy-blonde waves into a ponytail. Afterward, she grabbed her keys and purse, stopping a moment to check on the fledgling. The raven's eyes remained closed while Jade slipped into the fog.

She made her way outside, wincing at the chill in the air. The moon was bright, casting a silver glow over glassy waves. She hurried to the truck, eager to escape the breeze. Driving down the dark road, she headed to Pacific Grove.

Jade rubbed at her eyes, trying to push the drowsiness away. She was in desperate need of coffee if she was to stay awake before three o'clock. She took her turnoff, heading into the downtown area. Traffic was light. A couple of stray cats held council next to an overflowing dumpster in an alleyway. Their eyes glowed when the high beams exposed their hiding place.

Turning the corner, she noticed two police cars and a red fire engine parked in front of her shop. A group of firemen and patrol officers watched her climb out of the pickup truck. With key in hand, she headed over. A tall, dark-haired gentleman raised his hand in greeting.

"Jade Mackenzie?"

"Yes, that's me."

"I'm Aidan MacFie from the Pacific Grove Fire Department. The police are ready to investigate, but there doesn't appear to be any signs of a break-in."

"Oh, that's a relief."

"Good. So, they are going to secure the premises and then we'll take over to check for any signs of fire or smoke which might have set off the alarm. It's safer if you wait outside."

She nodded and wrung her hands, waiting to hear the news as first the police and then the firemen examined her property.

After what seemed like an eternity, the team came outside, the tallest of the three leading the way. He flashed a warm smile, helmet in hand.

"It's safe to enter now. Let's get you out of the cold."

The young man escorted Jade inside while the rest of the firemen headed back to their engine. The scent of potpourri and chimney smoke hung in the air, reminiscent of autumn.

The firefighter looked around the room, then moved closer to Jade.

"There doesn't appear to have been a fire, and there's no apparent damage. Perhaps there's something wrong with the alarm."

"You mean you got me out of bed at the crack of dawn for nothing?"

Aidan's brow rose as he studied the young woman, a flicker of amusement sparkling in his ocean blue eyes.

"Appears so, Miss Mackenzie."

She exhaled, trying her best to calm down. "Sorry. I...don't mean to be rude. It's not your fault. I'm half awake and this was a bit of a scare."

He considered her a moment, searching her face with interest. He flashed a lopsided smile and nodded.

"No worries."

"What did you say your name was again?" she asked, trying to make sense of her surroundings.

"Aidan MacFie."

He offered his hand, which she took. A tingling sensation warmed her skin. She was reluctant to let go but knew she must. Jade released his fingers and feigned a smile while stepping backwards.

The young man continued to watch her with the same curious expression.

"Seems like your day's not starting out for the best."

She shook her head, glancing out the window at the flashing lights outside.

"Guess not. Could be worse, I suppose. I'm preparing a grand opening for my shop. Would have been a disaster if there had been a fire or a break-in."

He looked around the spacious room at the unopened boxes and piles of antiques strewn across the floor.

"Looks like you have your work already cut out for you as it is."

"Yes, several packages arrived yesterday from a Carmel estate sale. It's going to be a challenge organizing everything."

"Well… I should leave you to it."

She studied his face in the soft morning light. He smiled down, dimples rising in the corner of his cheeks. Crystal blue eyes framed by long black lashes. The color reminded her of the sea—a startling aquamarine color. She'd never seen eyes so vibrant, almost unearthly in their clarity, and yet, they were strangely familiar.

She pushed a locket of sandy-blond hair from her forehead, while pulling her hoodie around her shoulders.

"Might want to check in with your alarm company today. They can take a better look at the equipment to see if there's any issues. The good news is there's no apparent damage to the property."

"Thank you. I'm sorry if I came across…impatient. Not quite my best without coffee."

He regarded her with a soft smile. Jade felt the heat rushing to her cheeks while she shifted her feet back and forth.

"Not a problem. That's what we're here for."

She couldn't shake the strange feeling of familiarity, as if they'd met before.

"Please call the station if anything comes up. It's just a few blocks over on Pine Avenue," he said.

"I'll do that."

When he was gone, she looked around the room and sighed. There was so much work to do to prepare for the store's unveiling.

Jade locked up the shop and headed back to the cottage for a shower and change. She got out of her truck a few minutes later to watch the ocean begin to reflect sunlight through her windows. It had been a long three months, but the shop was almost ready, and the cottage had been cleaned, cleared, and been transformed from a dusty refuge into a warm home. She smiled happily and entered.

After she'd showered and changed into a pair of jeans and a silk blouse, serenaded by the shrill cries of a young raven, she wrapped her damp hair into a lavender-colored bath towel. The raven was quiet while she moved the nest near the dining room window. The sun's rays formed diamond patterns through the lace curtains and across the kitchen countertops.

"Give me just five minutes, please," she said, in response to her pet's open mouth. She quickly found the approximate age for the bird and appropriate food. She set her phone down and nodded to herself.

The young woman offered the bird a piece of apple from the wooden bowl next to the nest. The fledgling devoured it in two gulps while watching Jade organize the morning meal. Vibrant snowy feathers ruffled as the raven's beak stretched in anticipation for breakfast.

"Alright, baby." Standing at the kitchen counter, Jade proceeded to mix grains, lentils, and honey into a marble mortar. She ground the concoction with her pestle, turning it into a rich paste.

After feeding her eager charge, she studied the bird with a gentle smile. Baby blue eyes flashed in anticipation.

"I think it's about time I named you." Sitting at the dining room table with her iPhone, she looked up articles on ravens.

"I'm going to take a guess that you're a girl by your size and attitude. You have a big personality, deserving of an important name." Celtic mythology was Jade's preferred method of finding an exotic sounding moniker that connected to her own heritage.

"Morrigan is a queen and protector of the earth in an Irish legend, a goddess of the land—both beautiful and powerful. You really are one-of-a-kind. A white raven is rare indeed. Would the name suit you, little one?"

The creature ruffled its feathers up like a tiny porcupine.

"Alright, Morrigan it is. Well, I'm going to be working at the shop late if I'm going to make my deadline. I think you better come too."

The raven tilted its snowy head and cawed in answer.

Jade gathered the nest and purse and headed back to the truck. After she picked up a café mocha and vegan Danish at the local drive-through coffee shop, they headed to work.

⚜

JADE PLACED MORRIGAN BY THE TABLE NEAR THE FRONT WINDOW TO ENJOY the sunlight. Afterward, she sat down cross-legged and began sorting through a box marked "fragile." While she was organizing vintage tea kettles and figurines, a sharp clatter emanated from the opposite end of the room.

Glancing up, she noticed the utility closet slightly ajar. Wincing from sitting too long, she moved towards the back of the room. She wiggled her right foot, trying to relieve the tingling sensation. She'd put much of the inventory that had come with the space in there, but she hadn't had time to go through it while collecting her own inventory and establishing contacts in the surrounding area. Knick-knacks, boxes, brooms, and cleaning supplies were all cluttered together behind the mahogany door. Turning the crystal knob, she pulled the partition fully open and peeked inside. A large rectangular package blocked the entrance. She reached down and freed it from the pile. It appeared to have fallen from the top shelf, knocking over several bottles in the process.

What on earth?

The young woman studied the package, biting down on her bottom lip. She'd poked around the broom closet several times and hadn't noticed it before. Jade brushed off a thick layer of dust before tearing the parchment away. Sunlight reflected the floating particles. Underneath was an oil painting encased in an ornate golden frame. She brought it over toward the front window. The canvas displayed a lone figure gazing towards a churning sea, gray seals reclining on the dunes nearby. The gentleman appeared to be in eighteenth century garb, wearing a formal Scottish kilt and leather boots. His sturdy back faced the viewer, his strong profile suggesting noble birth. Her heart raced when she studied the image. There was something familiar about the scene, but she couldn't quite place it. She reached for her phone, took a couple of photos of the painting, and sent them to her friend Mary.

Once she sent them, she called the number.

"Hello, you've reached The Muse Gallery, Mary Deane speaking."

"Mary, this is Jade Mackenzie."

"Oh, hey girl. How are you doing?"

"Pretty well. Just trying to get everything ready for the grand opening... feels like I'll never finish in time."

"Ugh, I feel your pain. You've been working down there on this for what, three months now? It's been almost a year since The Muse opened. I still have nightmares. I've been meaning to call you. Wanted to see if you needed help with your mom's house over here, since I've been keeping an eye on it. Looks like I'm covered at the gallery this week, so if you need help setting up, I can come down a few days early."

"Really? I would love that!"

"Great! Oh yeah, I have a friend in Napa who would be happy to come along. Runs a nursery business and is quite the artist. She collects antiques, so I imagine she'd love to check out your items. Her name's Katie O'Brien."

"Definitely invite her. The more the merrier. Hey, I just sent a couple of photos of a painting to your cell."

"Ok, I'll have a look. Is it one of the pieces from the estate sale you were talking about?"

"No, that's the funny thing. I don't remember purchasing it. I found the canvas this morning in the back of the supply closet. Really strange."

"That's odd. Maybe it was left from the previous owners?"

"Maybe. Well, anyways, I was wondering if you might have any idea of its age, or maybe the artist?"

"Sure. Let me look and see what I can come up with."

"Thanks so much. Looking forward to seeing you ladies this weekend!" Jade said.

After she hung up the phone, she propped up the canvas by the window. Something about the image struck her as familiar. She decided to bring it back to the cottage, maybe find a place to hang it.

Jade worked until lunchtime without a break. With her stomach rumbling and her face flushed from work, she placed the last antique teacup on the shelf and reached for her purse. She strolled along the avenues towards her favorite café. She chatted with the young barista, a teenager with a hot pink mohawk and an assortment of piercings as her mocha was brewed and her usual accompaniment arranged to be brought to her table.

A few minutes later, a gangly teenager delivered a bowl of lentil soup and a farmers' market salad to her seat. Jade blew away the steam from her mocha before taking a sip. She looked out the window and noticed a red engine parked outside.

The door opened with a blast of cool air and fall leaves. She glanced in surprise, recognizing the handsome firemen from her morning wakeup call.

Aidan MacFie placed his order, a large cup of coffee and blueberry scone, and then searched for an empty table. The corners of his mouth rose when he spotted Jade.

She motioned to the empty chair beside her.

"Thank you."

His friends leaned into one another and grinned, then took their coffee by the counter.

Aidan took a seat across from the young woman and sat back. Jade caught the whiff of light aftershave. There was another scent underneath, the fresh aroma of the sea.

"How's your day going so far? Better than this morning I hope?" Aidan said.

She played with her napkin while he studied her. "Pretty well, unpacked quite a few boxes, but I'm likely to be working into the night."

He studied her a moment without speaking, then he reached his fingers toward her face and her eyes widened. She held her breath as his hand grazed over, gently removing a piece of cobweb from her hair.

"Oh…thank you. Guess I should have checked the mirror before I left the shop."

"No worries. You're a busy lady." He smiled when she blushed.

"Do you live in town?" Aidan asked.

"Yes, I'm just a few miles down the road, not far. I recently inherited my grandmother's cottage. Still needs a bit of work, but it's lovely being so close to the beach."

"You don't happen to be talking about the cottage over by Ice Plant Lane?"

"Why yes, that's it," Jade said.

His eyebrows rose as he sat back in his chair.

"It really is a small world. I live close by. Probably passed your house a hundred times on my runs."

"Oh?" She perked up. "You're a runner?"

"Yes, mainly distance. And you?"

"I'm not fast but do enjoy long runs. Finished a couple of halves and completed the San Francisco Marathon last year." Shaking her head, she leaned back in her chair. "Oh boy, those hills are a killer." She let out a groan while she recalled the race. The last several miles were pure torture and she vowed never to run another marathon. Of course, she was already planning the next one soon after she'd crossed the finish line. Running was in her blood, and she prayed she'd always be able to enjoy the privilege.

"A marathon is quite the accomplishment. Good for you. I've completed a few triathlons. I enjoy running, but I'm more powerful in the water," Aidan said. He looked out the window and his brow knitted. "Sometimes I wonder if I can bring myself back to shore, I want to just stay afloat out on the waves." He turned back to Jade, realizing his mind was wandering. "I guess it's a silly notion."

"Not at all. I admire your devotion. I'm a terrible swimmer. Probably should get some lessons living so close to the water now and all."

"I'm sure you'd be a natural. If you're a runner, you already have the strength."

"Well…I don't know."

Jade glanced down at her hands, realizing there was dirt underneath her nails. She folded them onto her lap.

"I've always been a little nervous around the ocean. It's pretty to look at from a safe distance, but I'm not fond of being submerged." She looked up, fidgeting with the folds of her napkin. "I guess that probably sounds a bit odd," she said.

"Sometimes new things seem scary at first, and then before you know it, you're comfortable."

She studied his broad shoulders and chiseled profile. "Can't imagine you'd be afraid of many things."

His smile slowly faded. "Oh…you might be surprised."

He nodded when his coworkers approached. "Jade Mackenzie, this is Danny Green and Richard Rodriguez, my partners in crime." Both men were tall with muscular builds. Danny sported a striking red crewcut, his pale skin scattered with freckles. His teammate was slightly shorter with an olive complexion and dark brown eyes. They flashed admiring smiles at Jade.

"Guess we better be getting back to the station." Aidan drained his cup and stood up from his chair. "What time is your grand opening, lass?"

Lass? Was he joking? She studied his face while he waited for her answer. He appeared unaware that he'd said anything out of the ordinary, yet there was a sparkle of mischief in his aquamarine eyes.

"It's this Saturday from three to seven."

"I'll be finishing a forty-eight-hour shift early that morning, but I'll make it," Aidan said.

"Wonderful. And your friends are, of course, welcome. There'll be plenty of drinks and appetizers, and some prize drawings going on. Love to see you there."

After the men said their goodbyes, Jade sat back in her chair, studying the swirling patterns of foam in her coffee cup. The thought of Aidan stopping by the grand opening made her heart race. She paused a moment, looking out the window at the darkening sky. The handsome fireman had a Scottish surname, but she'd hadn't noticed the slight accent until now. She shook her head in amusement at being called *lass*. Not even her grandmother had ever called her anything like *that*.

She left a tip on the table and made her way outside into the hazy afternoon.

Morrigan cawed when she entered the store. For the next several hours, she concentrated on organizing and cleaning. When long shadows spread across the stone floors, she placed the last hand mirror on a shelf and smiled. Dust particles floated in the fading light by the window. Her favorite pieces were displayed on varying shelves and tables, adding to the vintage charm of the shop.

Jade walked over to the counter where her raven was resting, soft blue eyes flashing in the dimming light.

"Let's go home. I think we've done all we can tonight. I'm beat."

She grabbed her coat and keys and carried her charge to the truck, wincing as the wind struck her face. Clicking the radio to Macklemore's "Downtown," she drummed her fingers against the steering wheel while they drove toward the cottage.

She hurried over the cobblestone path, listening to the breaking tides. The fresh aroma of the sea invigorated her. For a moment, she stood in the doorway, studying the waves glistening beneath the silver moonlight. When she placed her key in the lock, a chill ran down her spine. A distant humming overlapped the rhythm of the sea. Jade tried to make out the sound but couldn't place it. After a few moments, the noise faded, so she turned toward the door and made her way inside. Morrigan chirped and stretched her pearly wings in anticipation of dinner.

After her pet ate a bowl of prepared grains and she had a generous salad, she poured a glass of Chardonnay. Glancing about the living room, she decided the painting would look best above the hearth. Strong gusts rattled the windowpanes while she prepared a fire. While the logs popped and crackled, she propped a small ladder beneath the mantel and proceeded to hang the canvas. Once it was secured, she climbed down and admired the painting. The imagery produced a mixture of excitement and trepidation. The lone figure standing by the shore troubled her somehow. There was something not quite right, but she couldn't lock down the source of her anxiety. She moved closer to the image. Her eyes narrowed as she studied a bundle resting near the man's boots. The surface appeared grey and slippery. Strange, she hadn't noticed it before.

Shaking her head, she put the ladder away and headed back to the kitchen to finish the dishes. Once she'd tidied up, she carried Morrigan and her nest to the bedroom. After washing her face and brushing her teeth, she slipped on a cotton nightgown and snuggled beneath the covers. Sleep came quickly that evening, but peaceful dreams were far and few.

❦

GLASSY WAVES COLLIDED AS JADE MOVED CLOSER TO THE SHORELINE. DAINTY feet sank beneath the wet sand. Before she realized it, icy water drenched her hips, soaking the ivory nightgown clinging against her chilled skin. She dared not go any further but knew she must. Maybe just a little more. Thunder boomed overhead while a fast-moving current pulled her forward. Her mind wandered for several moments in surrendered bliss. When she finally looked back at the shoreline, there was nothing but a pinpoint of land lost on the horizon. Realizing her danger, she panicked, flinging her arms wildly, swallowing a generous mouthful of salty water in the process. The frigid sea swept her further away.

Her body bobbed with the current, and then collapsed beneath the tide. Her mouth widened in a silent scream. Icy water filled her throat as she was pulled down to the murky depths. Once she succumbed to her fate, a peaceful silence embraced her soul. She blinked up toward the sky, confused by a brilliant wave of color. Hundreds of monarch butterflies fluttered above the sea, powdery black and orange wings blocking the rising sun. An unbearable pressure restricted her lungs. Her body was on fire while a thousand daggers pierced her chest. Her eyes flashed open as she began to rise to the surface, carried by powerful arms wrapping her in strength and protection. Together, they moved back toward the shore. After several deep chest compressions, a gush of water poured from her mouth. Coughing and heaving, she stared into vibrant blue eyes gazing down in panic.

"Jade!"

Chapter Two

Jade sat up in bed, heart pounding. The shrill cries of Morrigan brought her quickly back to reality. Pulling on a cotton robe, she left the warmth of her bed and headed to the kitchen. The soothing aroma of fresh espresso beans comforted her agitated mind. There was half a bowl of mash left over from the night before. She spooned the remainder of the seed paste for the eager baby.

Once breakfast was over, she changed into shorts and tank top, slipped on her running shoes, and made her way out into the thick fog.

When she neared the damp shoreline, fragments of the previous night's dream threatened her peace of mind. She jogged across the powdery sand while white caps capsized beneath shimmering tides. Ribbons of orange and pink mirrored the pounding waves. After a few minutes, her breathing evened out and she found her rhythm. Looking up toward the road, she noticed another jogger running the same direction. He spotted her from a distance and waved.

She studied him approaching, her eyes widening when she recognized the handsome fireman. He wore gray sweatpants with a white t-shirt clinging to his defined chest.

"Good morning, Jade." He spoke effortlessly while matching her strides.

"Morning." She sucked in her breath trying to keep pace.

"I've never run this part of the beach. There're 'No Trespassing' signs for over five miles."

"Yes, it's private property. My family purchased the rights over a century ago."

His eyes widened. "That's incredible. So, this all belongs to you?"

She nodded, trying her best to match his long strides. "You're welcome to run here anytime. Don't worry about the signs."

"Thank you. It would be a pleasure."

Aidan gave her an admiring glance as she made her way over the sandy shore.

He slowed his pace a bit so they could carry on a conversation. "I usually make my way down to the Fisherman's Warf area and follow the trails. This is much more…peaceful."

Jaded nodded in agreement.

"Yes, it's definitely my happy place. I try to take my runs by the ocean whenever the weather permits."

They edged closer to the tides, jogging in perfect synchrony. Icy waves rolled towards their feet; white sea foam splashed over their running shoes. She laughed, trying to dodge the water. He smiled down, dimples appearing in the corner of his cheeks. They decreased their strides when they neared tidepools and then slowed to a stop.

Jade put her hands on her hips and lowered her head to catch her breath. "Have you seen these before?"

"No…looks interesting."

They stood beneath a jagged overhang of granite-covered hillside. Colorful ice plants in striking pink and orange hues carpeted the cove. Several seagulls perched along the ledge, watching with interest as the couple approached the protected area. The waters were rich with sea life. Blue crabs scrambled about the shallow pools, grasping at swirling clumps of seaweed. One caught a silver minnow and took dainty bites of its prey. A second crab reached with its pincher, and then disappeared in a flurry of rising sediment. Tiny fish in varying colors darted in and out of polished caves, occasionally rising for food. Their upturned mouths formed question marks when they surfaced.

"It's really quite lovely…a hidden treasure," Aidan said.

"Yes, I love coming out here to gather my thoughts. It's relaxing watching the sea life."

"Oh, look! There's a starfish in the corner." Aidan pointed to a coral-colored creature hiding beneath floating plankton.

Jade giggled. "Looks like he's all alone. Poor boy needs a friend."

Aidan smiled down at her. She flushed, feeling his gaze, but continued to look out at the ocean rather than confront him. He seemed almost compelled, which she'd never experienced before. Finally, he turned away as if realizing he'd been staring. "You have quite a special area here. You mentioned you recently moved into the cottage?"

Jade bit down on her lower lip. "My mother passed earlier this year. She'd inherited my grandmother's home. Now it belongs to me. It seemed a shame to keep letting it lie fallow when I was moving here anyway."

Aidan reached down and took her hand in his. "I'm sorry. I know how difficult it is to lose a parent."

She saw the pain in his eyes and wished she hadn't broached the subject. "Oh...I'm sorry..." She didn't know what else to say.

He nodded, glancing up the hill. "Not sure about you, but I love a nice cuppa after a run. There's a Starbuck's about half a mile down the road. My treat if you'd like to join me."

"Oh, that sounds like heaven."

"Perfect." He paused a moment, studying her face. He seemed to want to say something, but then changed his mind and started jogging up the sandy hillside.

Jade tried to keep pace, but he had already reached the top by the time she was halfway up. She glimpsed his straining muscles and wondered how fast he could run if he really let loose. She slowed to a stop when she neared the sidewalk, placing her hands on her knees to catch her breath. When she looked up, Aidan smiled down, regarding her softly with aquamarine eyes. It would be so easy to lose herself in his gaze. Something about him made her feel safe and protected. She flushed while he watched her, wondering how she must look from running five miles without makeup.

"Great job! I'm sure that hill was a cakewalk compared to the San Francisco Marathon."

"Oh, a hill is a hill. I don't think I'll ever really enjoy them, but it sure feels nice on the way down." She grinned, looking forward to a strong cup of coffee and a chance to get acquainted with her new running partner.

"So true. They are a challenge." He chuckled, reaching for her hand. Once again, his gentle touch sent a bolt of energy through her body. After they approached the cafe, he released her fingers, somewhat to her disappointment. He flashed a smile, dimples rising in his cheeks.

"Coffee time?"

"Sounds good."

When they entered, they were greeted by the fresh aroma of expresso beans and warm pastries.

They ordered venti soy mochas and then took their seats by the window. The sky darkened, and the sound of low thunder rumbled in the distance. They were silent for a few moments while they sipped their drinks.

"So, how long have you been a fireman?"

"Seems like forever." He studied her flushed face and bit down on his bottom lip in thought. "I always wanted to…help people. Figured this would be the perfect way to do it."

She nodded. "Do you have family in the business?"

Aidan's jaw tightened at the mention of relatives. He shook his head and pretended to study something outside.

"No. I'm the only one." He looked down at his hands with a grimace.

"What about you? How long have you been working in antiques?" Aidan asked.

Jade played with her napkin, folding the corners until the paper was wadded in a tight square.

"Not long, really. But I guess you could say that it's in my blood. My great-grandmother ran a boutique in the nineteenth century in Monterey. She started the business shortly after traveling the Oregon Trail. It was actually her cottage originally, the one by the beach. They inherited the cottage from an elderly couple they'd met along the trail. My grandmother lived there for a while too. I wasn't expecting it to get to me for a while, but with my mom gone now…"

She blinked back hot tears and looked away. His large hands reached out and covered her petite ones. The touch was electric, and she looked up in surprise. His vivid eyes shone with compassion.

"I'm so sorry for your loss. I know how painful it is to be separated from loved ones, especially if it's unexpected or sooner than anticipated."

"Thank you."

They regarded one another in comfortable silence. She sensed he'd had his share of heartache but figured this was not the right time to explore it.

They chatted about happier topics for quite a while, but Jade noticed how he veered away from revealing anything too personal. She wasn't much for opening up about her own history but wondered why he seemed so guarded about his family. At the end of their coffee, she felt there was much left deliberately unsaid. While they strolled down to the beach, thick fog moved across the seashore. They made small talk as Jade studied Aidan's attractive features. She realized he could easily be a model with his pug nose, ocean-blue eyes, and perfectly white teeth. His body appeared Grecian in physique, broad chest, white t-shirt rippling over washboard abs. Yet, handsome as he was, there was a humbleness about him, a gentleness which permeated his every move. Before they knew it, they were standing before her cottage.

He studied the old place with his brows knit.

"Everything all right?"

Seeming to recover, he nodded. "It's just a funny coincidence. Your home…it's been part of this town for years and yet it's always been silent and lifeless." He smiled, but there was a hint of sadness in his eyes.

Jade didn't want to see him off just yet but was painfully in need of a hot shower and change of clothes.

"Would you like some more coffee?" she asked, gesturing inside.

He bit the bottom of his lip and considered her face. She waited as the cold wind reddened her cheeks and prickled at her steel-gray eyes. Aidan seemed to debate with himself internally, but in the end, simply grazed his fingers over her cheek, sending shivers down her body. She wondered if such a small touch could do that, what would it feel like if his hands explored elsewhere. The thought made her blush and she played with a loose curl, pushing it behind her ear.

He smiled down at her hopeful face.

"I'm starting my shift soon…I better get going."

Feeling somewhat foolish, she nodded.

"Of course."

He waved goodbye. She watched him make his way up the steep sandhill, disappearing into a blanket of fog.

She exhaled, walking up the cobblestone path. Once inside the cottage, she hurried to her closet, grabbed a new full set of clothes, and placed the whole pile on the shelf next to the antique clawfoot tub and shower. The mirror above the pedestal sink steamed over when she stepped inside. Warm water rolled down her back and she closed her eyes, releasing her breath. While the cotton washcloth moved over her skin, her thoughts moved to

Aidan, of Aidan's hands grazing over her body. Her breathing hitched as she allowed the fantasy to continue while the hot jets soothed her sore muscles and her mind drifted.

Finally, reluctantly, she left the warmth of the shower, wrapping herself up in an oversized towel. She dried off and dressed, and then headed to the living room. When she glanced up at the painting above the fireplace, her eyes widened in disbelief. *It's impossible*. She thought. *Was it the lighting?*

She stepped closer, standing on tip toes. The loan figure appeared closer to the shore.

That's crazy. Images in paintings don't move.

Shaking her head, she grabbed her purse and gathered up Morrigan along with her carrier. Fog drifted across a crimson sky. The wind whipped her blond waves across her face as she cradled the raven against her chest. A heavy mist blanked the truck's windows and rearview mirrors. With the wipers on high, she headed to Pacific Grove. Her mind was a tangled mess of confusion.

Chapter Three

THE WEEK LEADING TO THE GRAND OPENING WAS FILLED WITH ENDLESS projects. Jade's days were spent cleaning the shop, sorting through boxes, organizing merchandise, and hanging up paintings. Three more shipments arrived on Wednesday—including several valuable items from the Gilded Age. She placed a well-preserved nineteenth century copper tea kettle and a pewter candelabra near the front window. It caught the eyes of several tourists and locals. A sign outside announced the day of the grand opening. Reading her great-grandmother's diary inspired her to display a gold mining scene in the corner of the room. She'd ordered a couple of mannequins the month before. They arrived just in time for the party. Jade dressed the male in a corduroy shirt, Levi jeans, and old boots. She placed a gold mining pan in his large hands and stuck auburn whiskers to his chin and upper lip. When she was done, she studied the 49er with satisfaction.

Afterward, she carried a piece of plywood and set it on top of drop cloths. Jade set several cans of paints around the perimeter. Her fingers stroked the tip of her paintbrush while she readied herself. Morrigan cawed and flapped her wings, landing next to the sign.

She dipped her brush in the paint bucket and smiled, ready to unveil the name she'd chosen the day after moving in and signing her lease: Antiquities and Novelties of Pacific Grove.

Just as she was finishing painting a white raven logo in the corner, there was a light tapping at the front door. She stood up wincing; her right foot tingled from sitting so long. Jade smiled once she recognized the face of her best friend and her companion.

The bell chimed overhead as two women entered the shop.

"Mary, it's great to see you." She said, wrapping her friend in a bear hug.

"Jade, this is my friend I was telling you about, Katie O'Brien."

Mary was twenty-five years old with mahogany colored hair and a coiffed bob which caressed her slender shoulders. Her friend looked young as well, but there was a refinement in her features that hinted at hidden maturity. Auburn curls framed her profile and bright green eyes peered out beneath ebony lashes.

"So nice to meet you," Jade said. "Welcome! I apologize for the mess but make yourselves comfortable."

Katie and Mary entered the store, turning to admire the vintage items.

"Oh, your shop's beautiful!" Katie sighed while studying the teacups. "Are these Wedgwood?" she asked, emerald eyes widening.

Jade smiled and nodded. "Yes, I've been sorting through my new arrivals. Some of these are from the 1800s. You have a good eye."

"Thank you. Your pieces are breathtaking."

Mary carried a collection of canvases over to the front counter, stacking them carefully on top of the cherrywood. "Jade, I brought a couple of my paintings like you asked. They're part of a series I'm working on. Of course, they're not vintage, but definitely go along with your Gold Rush theme."

Jade examined the paintings. Together, they made a triptych. The first image displayed a middle-aged miner panning for gold over a rushing creek bed. The second painting was an early morning scene. A young cowboy chased after a rushing herd of long-horn cattle. The rider and animals appeared dangerously close to the edge of a cliff. The third canvas was of a frontier family enjoying supper in front of their covered wagon. An elderly man played the fiddle, while the younger members clapped.

"These are so beautiful! I know where I'll hang them." She pointed toward the corner by the front window. "They'll go perfectly with my gold mining display."

"Jade, you've been holding out on me," Mary said. "Who's this new man in your life?" She tickled the bottom of the manikin's burly beard and giggled.

"What's his name?" Katie asked.

"Hm…that's a good question," Jade said. She studied the miner with a soft smile.

"How about we call him…Joe…Joe Montana."

Katie nodded. "That's perfect! My favorite 49er of all time!"

"Mine too," Mary said.

"Maybe I should exchange his goldmining pan with a football?"

"Absolutely," Katie agreed.

The women giggled and patted the old miner.

Mary's brown eyes widened when she noticed the white raven.

"What on earth?"

Jade nodded and smiled. "Ladies, I'd like you to meet Morrigan. I found her outside my cottage. Figured I'd help her out while she heals."

"Such a pretty girl." Katie said.

Mary nodded and looked over at her friends. "I knew you two would get along famously. It's funny that you're both animal lovers and antique collectors."

Katie smiled at Jade. "That's wonderful!" She turned to look at the paintings on the wall. "A painter as well?"

"No…but I love art. Katie, I heard you're an artist," Jade replied.

"Yes, I dabble here and there when I get a chance. I'm not nearly as talented as our friend Mary. Have you visited her gallery lately?"

"Not since her grand opening. Been so busy with the new shop and cottage. I'd love to have you both over for dinner this weekend. I think you might be interested in a painting I recently acquired," Jade said.

"Yah, I'm curious to see the canvas in person. I did a bit of research after you texted me the photo. Appears to belong to the Romantic era. I might get a better idea if I saw it up close," Mary said.

"I'd love that," Jade said.

"We probably should check into our B&B. I believe it's on Ocean View Boulevard?" Katie asked, while checking her phone for the address.

"You're in for a treat. Most of those homes overlook the ocean. Maybe, we could meet up for dinner later after we unpack?" Jade asked.

The women nodded and smiled.

"Why don't you come by my cottage tonight for dinner? Mary, you have the address, right?"

"I do."

"Good. I'll make us some veggie pasta," Jade said.

Katie smiled. "Sounds perfect! I brought some fresh herbs and vegetables from home. I have plenty of heirloom tomatoes, Romaine lettuce, basil, and zucchini we can add. Mary mentioned you're a vegan, so figured you might enjoy them. I've plenty since I'm skipping the farmers' market this weekend."

"Oh fantastic! That will be such a treat. What do you say…maybe six tonight?" Jade asked.

"Perfect."

After Mary and Katie left the shop, Jade finished unpacking a box of vintage Depression-era drinking glasses and arranged them near an oak table by the register. She fetched a hammer, nails, and painting fasteners. After measuring Mary's paintings, she hammered fasteners into the wall and placed the triptych next to the gold mining display by the window. Satisfied, she collected her coat and raven and made her way into the foggy night. She drove to Monterey, stopping in at Whole Foods to collect some ingredients for their pasta dinner. After finding her necessary items, she picked out a Chardonnay and Cabernet along with a bouquet of autumn-colored flowers for the dining room table.

The wind whipped her hair over her face while she carried her groceries to the cottage. Once she'd started the fire and fed Morrigan, she organized ingredients for dinner. She'd just finished peeling and chopping a large garlic bulb when she heard a knock on the door. Jade and Mary were on the porch with their arms loaded with bags of fresh vegetables.

"Oh, what a gorgeous place!" Katie said.

"Absolutely adorable," Mary agreed.

"Thank you, ladies. Let me help you with those groceries."

"We brought tomatoes, lettuce, and pretty much everything you'll need for a salad. Oh, and of course some Napa Valley Chardonnay," Katie said.

Jade grinned. "You are so thoughtful! Thank you. I picked up some local wine myself. Great minds think alike!"

After the women organized the groceries, they wandered over to the fireplace and warmed their hands. Mary eyed the canvas above the mantel with curiosity.

"This is the painting you mentioned earlier?"

"Yes, I'd love your opinion on it," Jade said.

Mary opened her purse and retrieved a magnifying glass. Katie's brow rose and she giggled, shaking her head.

"I know...but one can never be too prepared. I learned that in Girl Scouts. Do you have something I could climb up on to get a better look?" Mary asked.

"Of course. Hold on just a second."

Jade fetched the ladder from the back closet and hurried over. Katie helped steady it while Mary climbed up. Her eyes widened when she studied the canvas.

"This is going to sound rather strange, but I swear the painting looks different from the one you sent me."

Jade sucked in her breath. "Believe me...it doesn't sound strange at all. I've had the same thought. It's almost seemed like the painting changed before my eyes."

Katie bit down on her bottom lip, steadying the ladder.

"May I have a look?"

Mary climbed down to make room for her friend.

"Well?"

Katie's smile slowly faded. "Sometimes things aren't always as they appear."

Jade nodded. "I'll try to keep an open mind. This is all so strange. I wish I had more facts." She studied their concerned faces and smiled. "This is getting way too serious. Should we get dinner started, ladies?"

The women nodded and followed Jade toward the modest kitchen and began organizing the meal. She reached for her favorite crystal glasses inside a cherrywood cupboard. "Beautiful antiques," Katie said.

"Thank you. My mom passed these down to me. They've been in the family for years."

She uncorked a chilled bottle of Chardonnay with a sharp pop. Jade filled the glasses while Mary and Katie gathered around in anticipation of a toast. The distant sounds of ocean waves echoed like background music.

Jade raised her glass. "To good friends, delicious food, and colorful mysteries."

"Cheers!" They cried in unison. When their glasses clinked, thunder erupted over head and a gust of wind shook the windows of the cottage. The lights flickered on and off. The women gasped then burst into giggles.

"I think I better light some candles," Jade said. "Just in case. The power is pretty sketchy here. The fireplace will definitely help if we lose power all together."

She walked toward the hearth to retrieve a vintage candelabra. The glow of the fire reflected off the recently polished pewter.

Jade placed it in the middle of the dining room table next to a vase of fresh wild sunflowers, lilacs, and roses. She returned with a box of matches and lit the candles. The aromas of fresh garlic and warm wax mingled together. They worked together for the next hour cutting, sautéing, boiling, and seasoning the dinner together as they chatted. While the rich scent of fresh tomato sauce filled the room, Jade set the table with her best china and crystal. Once the women had finished bringing bowls of food to the table, they took their seats.

Rain hit the tin roof as the wind shook the windowpanes. The friends sipped their wine as they talked, catching up on their business efforts, love lives or lack of, and general life struggles. After they'd put their dishes in the sink, the women took their glasses to the living room and continued their conversation. Once the rain let up, Mary and Katie called an Uber and headed back to their bed-and-breakfast.

Jade tidied up the kitchen after her friends said their goodbyes. She tucked in Morrigan for the night. When she'd brushed her teeth and undressed, she took a seat by her vanity.

The Nineteenth century antique was one of her most cherished possessions along with a silver brush and comb set that belonged to her great-grandmother. Holding it in her hands always made her feel connected to the past. It was like a hug from her ancestor. She ran the brush through her golden waves, listening to the surf hit the shore. Satisfied, she slipped into her four-poster bed. Jade enjoyed a few chapters of *Pride and Prejudice* before drifting into a peaceful night's sleep.

Chapter Four

FOR THE NEXT TWO DAYS, JADE FOCUSED ON THE FINISHING TOUCHES FOR the grand opening. Katie and Mary took turns unpacking boxes, creating price tags, and taking turns running errands. The last few hours of preparation were crazy, but they ended up finishing just in time. An impressive line of people waited outside in anticipation. They'd set up a champagne station, a second table filled with vegan appetizers, and a third with desserts and coffee. A nineteenth century Irish tea set was on display by the front window. Customers were invited to enter the raffle when they entered the shop. There was plenty of foot traffic that afternoon and soon the store was filled with enthusiastic buyers peppering Jade with questions.

An hour into the party, a petite elderly woman approached the register with a porcelain teapot. Her ebony eyes glistened with excitement while Jade wrapped up her treasure. The corners of her mouth lifted when she noticed the white raven.

"Your bird is very beautiful."

"Thank you," Jade smiled down at the customer, noticing her crooked stance, and pained expression. "Her name is Morrigan. She was injured when I found her but seems to be attached to me even though she's healed up nicely."

The fledgling watched the woman with interest, spreading her pearly wings outward. The raven closed her eyes as the elderly lady stroked her head.

"Animals have a way of knowing who means them well. Don't they, dear? Just like spirits."

Jade's hands froze on the sides of the package. Her skin felt like it had been submerged in ice water.

"I'm sorry?"

"Well, when you've been on this good earth for as many years as I, you learn some interesting things." She smiled, considering the young woman's expression. "Are you a religious young lady?"

Oh, here we go, Jade thought, imagining the woman was going to try to hand her a pamphlet about the end of the world.

"Umm...I'm Catholic. Been missing quite a few Masses the last several months. Probably should try to make the time," she said in a light-hearted tone.

The elderly lady moved closer and reached her hand over the countertop.

"Make the time, dear. I feel a presence around you."

Jade winced, feeling the customer's fingers graze over the back of her wrist. Knotty veins protruded beneath crepe skin, not unlike clusters of purple spiderwebs. The woman turned Jade's hand palm up and let out her breath.

"Interesting. Your lifeline reveals some interesting things, dear."

She studied Jade with a benevolent smile, while her ebony eyes flickered in the darkening room.

Jade pulled her hand back slowly, trying her best not to offend her customer.

"Perhaps you'd like to learn more?"

Jade's eyebrows rose in question.

"I offer palm and Tarot card readings in my home. You're welcome to come by any time. I'm just a few houses down the road," she said, pointing toward the window behind the register.

"Oh, thank you. I'm not really into that kind of thing, but I appreciate the offer," Jade said. She studied the senior citizen's wrinkled face, hoping she hadn't hurt her feelings.

Her gnarled hands gathered the package from the counter.

"Very well, dear."

Katie noticed the elderly woman heading toward the door.

"Would you like some help carrying your purchase?"

"Oh, what a dear girl! Yes, please."

She smiled and escorted the customer outside.

"What was that about?" Mary asked.

"I'm not completely sure. We were talking about Morrigan and the next thing I know she's warning me about spirits."

"Spirits?"

"Yep."

"That's pretty spooky."

"Ya think?" Jade laughed, shaking her head. "She invited me to her home for a palm reading. I've had a few crazies hanging outside the store this week. I met one gentleman insisting he was Salvador Dali... reincarnated, of course!"

"Of course!" Mary said. "I guess it's goes along with running a business. You get all kinds."

"I'm sure she's just a superstitious old woman. Who knows," Jade said.

Katie came back into the shop with the jingle of the bell above her head.

"Mrs. Garnier asked me to give you this." She handed Jade a business card.

Madame Jane Garnier - Medium and Demonologist
Specializing in the Occult - Multi-dimensional Traveler
Tarot and Palm Readings by Appointment.
Visa and MasterCards Welcome.

Jade shook her head and filled in Katie about their conversation.

Katie looked between her friends and sighed.

"You know, I would have laughed it off a year ago, but I've had my share of strange happenings. You'd probably have me locked up if I told you half of the things going on since I moved to Napa."

"Oh?" Mary said.

Katie looked down at her small hands and smiled. "Well...there's been so much good mixed with the bad." Jade noticed how she played with her engagement ring with her right hand. Mary's brow raised.

Katie looked back at her friends and smiled. "Try to keep an open mind. I've had to learn that lesson the hard way."

Jade let out a breath, trying to put on a brave face despite the elderly woman's ominous warning.

"Thank you. There have been a few strange occurrences since I've moved into my home. Sometimes I swear I'm not alone at the cottage. There's strange noises out at sea."

Mary bit the corner of her lower lip. "What do you mean?"

"It's almost always at night. There's a distant sound of whispering. It's impossible of course, but I swear I hear it. Sometimes I'll be reading or drifting off to sleep when I notice a keening coming from the shore. It builds in crescendo, and then drifts into a haunting requiem." Jade crossed her arms over her chest. "Crazy, right?"

Mary and Katie exchanged concerned glances.

A bell jingled over the brass doorway when Aidan made his way inside the shop. He was dressed in a pair of tan trousers and a navy-blue silk shirt and tie. The color complimented his eyes. The women smiled while he made his way over with his hands behind his back. He bowed toward Jade, and then offered his radiant smile. He presented her with a large bouquet set in an ornate crystal vase.

Her mouth fell open, studying the lavish gift.

"Good afternoon, ladies. Looks like your grand opening really brought in the tourists today." He looked around the room, admiring the turnout. "Jade, I wanted to bring you a little something to celebrate your special event."

Her friends glanced at one another and smiled as she took the vase in her arms.

"Oh, they're beautiful! Thank you."

She felt the heat rising to her cheeks, so she breathed in the fresh aroma of roses and lilacs and admired the flowers while Aidan's blue eyes flickered in the fading light.

"Oh, you shouldn't have. My gosh…the vase alone looks priceless. It's so unique…almost presents like Georgian glass, but I know that would be almost impossible."

"Oh, you have a good eye. It's a little something from my own collection."

She glanced up, dumbstruck.

"Georgian?" she whispered.

He smiled and nodded. "It's one of my favorites, but I'd like you to have it."

She started to protest, uncomfortable for accepting something so valuable from someone she barely knew, especially when she'd heard stories of expectations and abusive relationships starting out with lavish gifts, but something in his eyes prevented her. There was a hopeful, honest look that begged to be accepted.

Jade looked around. "Aidan, I'd like you to meet my friends Mary and Katie."

"Pleasure to meet you." He took turns shaking their hands and making introductions.

Katie glanced at Mary with a knowing smile.

"Looks like there's a few customers in the back room that need help with some paintings," Mary said. She linked arms with Katie and whispered something in her ear. The women giggled and made their way to the back of the store.

"Would you like a glass of champagne?" Jade asked.

"Thank you."

She went to the back storeroom and retrieved a bottle from the cooler. She carried it out to the counter.

"May I?" Aidan asked.

"Please."

His large hands wrapped around the cork and he flicked it effortlessly. A burst of foam spilled over the bottle and Jade laughed placing the flutes on the counter and grabbed a towel. She poured them each a glass while he watched her expectantly.

Their fingers grazed when she handed him his flute. An electrical feeling resonated from his touch, the same way it had the day by the beach.

"To your grand opening. *Lang may yer lum reek.*"

Jades eyes widened in question.

"It's a Scottish saying which means 'I wish you well for the future.'"

"Thank you. That's very beautiful. Are you Scottish, Aidan?"

"Yes, my parents were from Scotland. I haven't been back for some time. It is a lovely country."

Jade sighed. "Oh, I've always wanted to visit. I've never been abroad."

His eyes twinkled and he stepped closer, placing his hand beneath her elbow.

"Aye, with a name like Mackenzie, ye need to visit the Highland Hills. Find where you hail from."

She giggled at his accent. "Oh, I'd love to, but I wouldn't know where to even start."

Aidan took a sip of champagne, searching her face. "Well, if ye ever need a tour guide, I'd be up to the challenge." He offered his lopsided grin, aqua-marine eyes sparkling in the fading light.

"I think I'd like that," Jade said.

He grinned, looking around the room with interest. "Pretty busy?"

"Yes. It's been a wonderful turnout so far. Although…I did have a rather unusual customer," she said. The bubbles tickled her nose as she sipped from her glass.

"Oh?"

"An elderly woman stopped by earlier. She was quite mysterious…like a character from a book or something."

"Really?"

"She was sweet. Purchased one of my favorite teapots. But there was something about her that really gave me the strangest feeling. Not quite sure what she was really trying to convey. She spoke in riddles, implying there was something unnatural in my shop." She looked down at the floor, uncertain if she should say more.

Aidan stepped closer, gently tilting her chin up.

"What else did she say?"

Jade blinked, trying to recall her words, distracted by his gentle touch. "She started off by asking about my religion."

A smile moved over his handsome face.

"Fair question. What was your answer?"

"I said I was Catholic but hadn't been to Mass for a few months with setting up the shop and all. I haven't even had a chance to find a new church since the move."

"Oh? There's a lovely Catholic church just down the road on Lighthouse Avenue."

"Saint Angela's?"

"Yes, that's the one," Aidan confirmed.

"I've driven by it several times."

"It's a nice cathedral."

"Are you Catholic?"

"I am, but I'm guilty of missing church myself the past few months. Maybe we could drop by together one of these Sundays."

"Yes, I'd love to." She smiled, considering his face. He was full of surprises and Catholic, too? *Mom would have loved him. Scottish too, so grandad wouldn't even complain.* She bit the bottom of her lip trying to stay focused.

"So, back to the elderly woman. What else did she have to say?" Aidan asked as he leaned on the counter.

"She felt a presence in my shop and said I should be careful." Jade rubbed her shoulders as a chill ran down the back of her neck. "Gave me the creeps."

His hand moved from her face to her shoulder. A warming sensation tingled over her skin. All her anxiety melted at his touch.

"Do you have your phone nearby?"

She looked up puzzled. "Um...yes. It's behind my desk."

"Let me give you my number," Aidan said.

She reached for her phone, trying her best not to seem too eager. His breath tickled against her skin and she tried to focus on the keyboard to type it correctly while seeming nonchalant.

"If you get nervous at the shop or cottage just give me a call. Don't hesitate—day or night."

She looked up into his aquamarine eyes and her breath hitched. He continued talking, but she barely heard him. Instead, she focused on the vibrant color. The sound of piercing screams snapped her back to reality. They both turned to hear the cries of a mother and her misbehaving son. Jade groaned to herself, rushing over. Aidan followed close behind.

"Timmy! Get down from there this instant!"

A young child clung to the manikin. The pan and gold nuggets teetered in the air. While the boy rocked back and forth, the mining shovel slipped to the floor with a loud bang. A jar of pyrite followed, shattering glass and gold dust onto the ground. His mother reached her plump arms toward her misbehaving child. He ignored her and proceeded to stick out his tongue. The boy giggled, climbing even higher.

"Get down!"

Jade sucked in her breath, realizing the display was dangerously close to toppling over.

Timmy kicked the sides of the miner like a bucking bronco, then inched himself upwards. Once his feet wrapped around the shoulders, gravity took

over. Aidan caught the child just inches from landing face-first onto the stone floor.

The boy stared up at Aidan, his bottom lip trembling.

"Careful, lad. Ye almost plummeted on yer head."

The child's mouth trembled as his face dissolved into a mask of tears. He rubbed his eyes with the back of his hand while his mother pulled on the other. The pair hurried outside, and the boy's sobs echoed down the street.

Jade looked to Aidan and sighed. "Thank you. He could have really hurt himself."

"Not a problem, lass."

Lass? There it was again, she thought. He didn't have a trace of an accent when they'd first met, but this was the second time it slipped out.

Aidan moved the mannequin back into position while Mary and Katie swept up the broken glass and chunks of fool's gold. Jade wheeled over a trash can for the sweepings.

"I guess I was tempting fate with the gold mining display. The children have been making beelines to it the minute they enter the store."

"The mannequin looks authentic," Aidan said, running his hand over the tin pan with a faraway look. "Of course, gold miners really never used the picks as much as the shovels."

"Interesting. I didn't realize that you knew so much about the 49ers," Jade said. "That's not common knowledge."

Aidan realized everyone's eyes were on him and offered a disarming smile. "Oh, I must have heard it somewhere. Probably from one of those history channels."

Jade studied him, sensing he was holding something back. *Strange,* she thought.

Once the crowd dispersed, Aidan moved towards the front window. Garnet rays stretched over the heavens while a blanket of fog darkened the ruddy sky.

"Looks like another storm is brewing," he said.

Jade stood next to him, studying the threatening cloud cover. "It sure does."

He smiled down, locking eyes with Jade. Then, realizing her friends were watching, he moved towards the door.

"It's been lovely meeting you all." He nodded toward Katie and Mary. "Should probably finish up some errands before heading home."

He glanced out the storefront window watching the sky turn to dusk.

"Tomorrow's going to be another long day," Aidan said.

"Oh?" Katie questioned with a sidelong glance.

"Yep, my schedule can be pretty grueling at times. At least we don't have to contend with a full moon for a few more weeks. It's crazy how the lunar pull can affect people. There's always more emergencies when it happens, so my team's work usually doubles," he said.

"Oh, well thank you for making the time to stop by. The flowers and vase are so lovely," Jade said sincerely.

He offered his lopsided smile. "My pleasure, darlin'." He started for the door, and then turned back toward Jade. His face grew serious while he regarded her. "Don't forget…if anything's worrying you, here or at the cottage, don't hesitate to call."

"Thank you, Aidan."

"You're welcome, darlin'." The bell jingled over his head when he left the shop and a trail of autumn leaves blew across the floor. A gusty wind fluttered the lace curtains against the front window. Once he was gone, Jade's guests huddled around her smiling.

"Well?"

"Well what?" Jade said. She tried her best to hide her growing infatuation.

"Where did you meet that gorgeous fireman," Mary asked, fanning herself with her hand. She moved closer, eager for news.

Jade let out a sigh and smiled. She quickly filled them in on the mysterious morning last week the shop's alarm went off.

Katie brushed her auburn curls out of her emerald eyes. "There's a bit of an accent when he talks…but not all the time. My fiancé's Irish, but his brogue never changes."

"Yes, I've noticed. Aidan's a private person. It's been a bit tricky getting to know him. He has a habit of dancing around any mention of his family or past. He told me he's lived in town for some time, but also said his parents are from Scotland and he's been there."

"Interesting, a man of mystery," Mary said speculatively.

"Yes, he's definitely that." Jade shook her head as a smile spread over her face.

"Do you have any plans to see your friend again?" Katie asked.

"Well, we did meet up on a run earlier this week and went to coffee afterward. And I mentioned my encounter with Madame Garnier this afternoon. Told him what she said really gave me the creeps. He gave me his number before he left the shop."

"Wow. It might be handy to have Aidan on speed dial. Bet he could be right over whenever you're in need," Mary said slyly. "Even break down the door."

Katie laughed while shaking your head. "Mary, you're terrible!"

Jade blushed at their gentle teasing. "Oh, it's nothing like that. I'm sure he's just being kind."

"I bet he's extremely kind…and giving. No doubt," Mary said.

Katie giggled watching Mary wiggle her eyebrows.

Jade smiled to herself, wondering what it might be like to have a private assistance from the handsome Scotsman. She sighed at the scenarios flashing through her mind. When her final customer left the store, Jade switched her sign from "Open" to "Closed" and waved her friends over to the counter. She opened the last bottle of champagne and filled their flutes.

"I want to thank you for all your support today. The grand opening was quite the success, even with Joe Montana nearly broken in two! I was thinking we could Uber around town tonight. I'd love to take you to dinner. My treat. There's a wonderful vegan café just down the street. Maybe we could visit an Irish pub afterward?"

Katie and Mary nodded. "Sounds like a date!"

"Perfect! Do you mind if we drop off Morrigan at my cottage first?"

"No problem," Mary replied.

After they'd set up Morrigan for the night, Jade ordered an Uber. Ten minutes later, a middle-aged woman pulled up in the driveway. She opened the back door to her Honda Civic and smiled. The women chatted while they drove toward downtown.

Chapter Five

THE FRIENDS WERE STARVING BY THE TIME THEY ARRIVED AT THE restaurant. The Rainbow Café was a local hotspot for tourists and locals. Colorful ocean scenes by local artists were hung on the brightly colored walls. The shop owner, Janice Darby, greeted Jade by name and seated them at a table by the window.

"Drinks, ladies?"

"We'd love to start with a bottle of your best Chardonnay," Jade said.

The owner smiled and returned shortly with three glasses and a chilled bottle of wine.

"It's a good thing we have a driver tonight. I'm going to need to be carried by the time we're finished," Mary said.

"Agreed." Katie sat back in her chair and sighed.

Once their glasses were filled, Jade raised hers in the air. "Thank you for your help today, ladies. I couldn't have done it without you. Your support means the world to me."

The women took turns toasting and congratulating Jade on her successful store opening.

After dining on a delicious combination of soy polenta and brown rice dripping in rich garlic sauce, the ladies shared slices of carrot cake and chocolate torte. Once they finished their meal, Jade paid for dinner and thanked the owner. The friends walked a few blocks down Lighthouse

Avenue to visit a local Irish pub. The owner of the Blarney Stone, a middle-aged woman with salt-and-pepper hair, was announcing over the speaker that Trivia Night was about to start just as they came in. The ladies took their seats by a table near the front window and quickly agreed to log as a team. Each patron was offered sheets of paper along with a pen. The subjects ranged from history to current affairs. By the end of the night, they'd tied points with a team of men in their early thirties. Their impressive man buns and thick beards made Jade think of the team as "the hipster table." While they discussed the questions, the men stole admiring glances at their opponents.

Near the end of the evening, the pub's owner reached down from her podium and retrieved a framed print. She held the back of the painting toward the audience and smiled.

"Well, this has been a competitive group tonight! It appears we have a tie between two tables. It's ladies against the men. Our final question will have a visual component."

The women exchanged looks, wondering what it might be.

"The first to raise their hand and successfully answer the correct artist and subject of the portrait will be the winner. Any questions?"

The room was quiet, so she proceeded. She turned the image toward the audience. A smile played over Mary's face when she recognized the dark eyes and hair of the woman in the painting.

"I'd like the name of the artist. You'll receive an extra bottle of wine if you guess the title," the owner said.

Mary's hand shot up and her friends looked at her with wide eyes.

"That was mighty fast, miss. What is your answer?" the owner asked, unable to keep the joviality from her tone.

"The artist is Édouard Manet and the subject of the painting is artist Berthe Morisot. The portrait was completed in 1872 and the title is *Berthe Morisot with a Bouquet of Violets*. Both artist and subject were prominent leaders in the Impressionist Movement in Paris in the nineteenth Century."

The men at the competing table glanced over with their mouths hanging open.

"Very good! It appears we have an art historian in the house. You not only named the subject and artist but knew the title and date. You're the winner of tonight's gift basket featuring a collection of our tavern's favorite local wines. Congratulations!" The owner hefted up the sizable basket and motioned for the women to come up to the front of the pub. The members of the hipster table clapped and whistled while the ladies accepted their prize.

The pub owner offered the microphone to Mary. "Any words you'd like to say?"

She smiled out at the crowd. "It just goes to show: an art history degree can come in handy every now and again!"

Laughter broke out, followed by more applause. The women giggled as they left the tavern. They shivered in the frigid air as Jade phoned in an Uber and waited with her friends under a covered awning.

"Great job, Mary!" Katie said.

Jade nodded. "I think we make a pretty good team."

⊛

MARY AND KATIE SAID THEIR GOODBYES AFTER THEIR UBER PARKED OUTSIDE their bed and breakfast.

"I can't wait for your next visit, ladies. Thanks again for all of your help this week," Jade said.

"You're so welcome," Katie said.

"I might have some more free time in a couple of weeks. Jade, why don't you take our gift basket to your cottage. Except for...this one," Mary said, plucking out a bottle. "I'll need this to tackle the issues I'm sure to face when I get back. But that way we can share the wine on our next visit. Do you want to keep one, Katie?" Mary asked.

"No, I think it's a great idea to have Jade guard them all. Besides, it's something to look forward to. My fiancé is picky about his alcohol," Katie said.

Jade nodded in agreement. "Hope you have a safe drive back. See you soon!"

The women said their goodbyes, promising to get together in a few weeks. The Uber driver played soft jazz on the radio while they drove through the thick fog. Jade struggled to keep her eyes open on the ride home. She stifled a yawn before closing the passenger door. Once inside the cottage, she flicked on the lights and checked on Morrigan.

"Did I wake you, sweetie?"

The bird's eyes fluttered and closed; her pale feathers ruffled as she settled into her nest. Jade slipped out of her clothes and washed her face.

After she'd changed into her pajamas and robe, she prepared a mug of cocoa before making her way to bed.

Morrigan's pearly head was tucked under her wing, fast asleep. Slivers of moonlight slipped through her lace curtains while Jade listened to the waves hit the shore. She reached for her novel by the bedside and snuggled beneath the quilts.

After reading the same sentence from Jane Austen's *Pride and Prejudice* for the third time, she placed her book on the nightstand and turned off the Tiffany lamp by her bed. The evening storm lulled her to sleep. Gentle raindrops turned to hail; a heavy wind shook the cottage's foundation. Jade shivered as icy air made its way underneath the door and snuggled deeper beneath her blanket.

ﷺ

DAINTY FEET SANK INTO THE WET SOIL AS SHE NEARED THE SHORELINE. THE light scent of heather hung in the air. Before she knew it, salty water was brushing her hips while she listened to the sounds of the sea—a hypnotizing lullaby which drew her forth.

From within the infinite waters emerged a dark form. While Jade moved through the soft bands of moonlight, her eyes caught sight of a gray mass rising from the tides. She blinked in wonder watching the foaming currents wash over the mysterious beast. The creature's flesh pulsated; scarlet droplets oozed from its pores. A red line sliced through the back of the animal, sloughing off blubber and grey meat. Once freed from the slippery hide, a young man wiggled forth from the confines of the encasement.

He stretched out his muscular arms in a wide arch, long legs moving through the water with ease. His appealing physique was nude and perfect. The powerful body dove beneath the raging waters and then emerged from the frothy tides glistening with seafoam. Dark curls fell over his eyes and he swam toward her. She knew his face, and her heartbeat drummed in anticipation. Her mind tried to make sense of what she was seeing. He beckoned her with outstretched arms.

Jade lifted her dress to her thighs and kicked her way toward him, heart thumping in anticipation. They gazed at one another in mutual longing. He pulled her close, their lips melding together, fingers trailing over supple skin. His tongue darted inside her mouth while he pulled her closer. She met his desire head on, wrapping her arms around his neck. He held her in his protective embrace, keeping her anchored within the churning sea. Her head relaxed against his chest as he paddled water. She watched as the shoreline fell away until it was a distant pinpoint of land. A feeling of sublime peace radiated through her body. His tongue flicked over her heaving bosom. She bit down on her lower lip in ecstasy. Moonlight flickered in his aqua-marine eyes.

"I want you," she whispered.

His mouth pulled up at the corners.

"I've always loved you, lass. I've been waiting for so long."

She closed her eyes, inhaling the aroma of the sea. When she opened them, he was gone. Jade turned in panic toward the shore, but there was nothing left but darkness.

Chapter Six

JADE SAT UP IN BED, A COLD SWEAT CLINGING TO HER SKIN. HER HANDS were shaking as she switched on the light by the bedside. She glanced towards her dresser and gasped, realizing Morrigan was missing from her usual perch. As she slipped on her slippers and robe, a loud cawing sounded from the living room.

"Morrigan?"

She hurried over, smiling when she spotted her pet sitting above the fireplace mantel, pale blue eyes flashing in the morning light.

"Oh, thank goodness. There you are, baby."

The raven flapped her pearly wings and let out her high-pitched caw.

"Decided to do a little exploring today? You scared me half to death, little one."

The young woman released her breath and the bird flew to her shoulder. Morrigan immediately began preening Jade's sandy-blond curls. She stroked the bird with a trembling hand.

"You must be growing nicely if you made it all the way here."

She giggled as her pet nestled its face against her flushed cheek.

"Better get you your breakfast after your adventure."

She started to turn toward the kitchen then froze in her tracks. A puddle of water was in front of the hearth. She leaned down on her haunches to inspect closer.

"How did that get there?" Her gray eyes widened; she followed a trail of sandy footprints leading to the front door. They were petite in size, like her own. She swallowed, her breath hitching in her throat.

"I don't understand." She talked aloud to the empty cottage.

The young raven chirped backed in response. Jade's eyes raised up, resting on the portrait. The lone figure stood by the seashore; an ominous shadow now appeared not far behind. A clump of gray matter appeared to have washed ashore.

This isn't happening. It must be a prank. Her mind tried desperately to make sense out of the chaos. She studied the painting in disbelief, still groggy from her strange dream. In need of coffee, she rushed to the kitchen, cradling her raven. Soon, the rich aroma of expresso beans filled the cottage. She poured herself a generous mug, mixing in a bit of almond creamer. There was leftover seed paste from the night before which her charge greedily devoured. Desperately needing fresh air, she made her way out to the porch. Jade placed her coffee on an oak table by the wooden swing. After she took her seat, her eyes spotted a large brown-paper package resting on the bottom of the stairs. She stepped down, heart racing. When she reached for the parcel tied with string, a tightening sensation clawed at her throat and she froze as the odor of something rotten buffeted her. Out of the corner of her eye a man appeared jogging across the dunes. Startled, Jade turned in his direction. Her eyes widened as he headed her way.

"Aidan?"

"Morning, Jade. I apologize for stopping by unannounced. I tried to call earlier to see if you wanted to go for a run. When you didn't answer, I took the liberty of heading over. Hope I'm not interrupting anything?"

Aidan came to a stop, his smile fading when he noticed the young woman's pale face.

"Is everything all right?"

Tears welled in her gray eyes; she tried to find the words.

"No, not really. Things are a mess. I…don't even know where to begin."

He placed his hand on her shoulder and smiled.

"Why don't you start at the beginning?"

She nodded and took a deep breath. "All right, but you're going to think I'm a lunatic when I'm finished."

He grinned. "I doubt that."

"Would you like a cup of coffee?"

"Sure."

"Why don't you have a seat on the porch swing. I'll be right back."

Jade went inside to prepare his beverage. A few minutes later, she appeared with a thermos of coffee, a pitcher of almond milk, and a bowl of sugar.

Aidan moved to open the door while she balanced the serving tray.

"Thank you." She placed their coffee on a small table by the porch swing.

"Sugar?"

"Pardon?" He smiled up at her.

She took a breath to steady herself. "Would you like some sugar with your coffee?"

"Oh, yes please."

Jade spooned sugar into his mug along with a splash of almond creamer. She handed him his drink and leaned back in the swing. Aidan was quiet a moment while she gathered her thoughts.

The raven perched on her shoulder, cocking her head toward the handsome fireman.

"Aww, there's the little lass I saw at your shop. She's bonnie."

"Thank you. Morrigan's been a real joy to have around." Jade set down her cup and turned toward Aidan. "So, there's been some very odd things happening at both my cottage and the shop." Jade explained the changes in her painting and the odd sounds she'd been hearing at night. She mentioned some details of her dreams but refrained from adding the erotic elements. Aidan frowned at the package, making a face at the pungent aroma.

"I'm guessing this is one of those strange things?"

"Yes."

"What do you suppose it is?"

"I have no idea. It was outside my door this morning."

"Would you like me to open it?" Aidan asked.

"Oh, I hate to ask you. It smells rotten."

"It surely does, but we need to know what we're dealing with here. There's only one way to find out."

Jade nodded and sighed. "Thank you. I don't think I could touch it."

He reached into his sweatpants' pocket and withdrew his pocketknife. The blade tore through the taut string then he pulled back the parchment.

Maggots twisted and churned over a mass of slippery gray flesh. Aidan's jaw clenched as he studied the contents.

Jade covered her mouth with her hands. "Oh my god…what is it?"

"Appears to be animal remains." He took a deep breath, letting it out slowly.

Jade's eyes filled with tears. "It looks like seal skin. The poor thing. Who would do such a thing? Wasn't this outlawed ages ago?"

"I'm not sure, but we need to report this." Aidan placed his hand gently over Jade's shoulder. "Let's bring this to the police station. I think you should meet Sheriff Carpenter. He's a friend of mine. This needs to come to the attention of the authorities. People aren't allowed to trespass on private property or leave threatening packages."

"Let me just gather my things and we can go over," Jade said.

"All right."

"Why don't you wait inside while I get ready?"

Aidan nodded and followed her into the cottage.

"Your home's beautiful," he said. He moved over to the fireplace, glancing above the mantel. "Is this the painting you were talking about?"

"Yes. I swear the figure moves every day."

"Interesting."

Jade studied his face, trying to determine if he believed her. There was a hint of sadness in his eyes that wasn't there before. She wondered what he was thinking but was afraid to ask.

"I'll be right back. Make yourself comfortable."

"Thank you."

When Jade returned, she found Aidan standing close to the painting. He was biting his bottom lip and studying the man in the shadows looking perturbed.

Aidan turned when she came back in. She was holding her purse and jacket but felt braver and composed in a Kelly-green skirt with a matching silk blouse with her sandy blond locks gathered into a high ponytail. The color in her cheeks returned, along with the sparkle in her eyes.

"I'm ready."

"Perfect," Aidan said, placing his hand on the small of her back and escorting her to the door.

Once inside the truck, Jade switched on the radio. "Do you have any preferences?"

"Whatever you like."

She punched in her favorite hip-hop station, tapping her fingers on the steering wheel. Rihanna's latest hit brought a smile to her face. A few moments later, they turned onto Pine Avenue.

Jade followed his directions until he said, "Go ahead and take a right here and park in the back."

After they'd parked the truck, Aidan removed the box from the backseat and carried it to the door. To their relief, the normally busy office was quiet that morning. A woman in her mid-thirties shuffled papers as they made their way to her desk. She wore a navy-blue blazer and pencil skirt donned with red-bottomed heels. The receptionist absently twirled a lock of bleach-blonde hair while she studied her computer screen. Her soft blue eyes widened when she noticed Aidan.

"Hello, Tiffany. Is Sheriff Carpenter in today?"

"Good morning, Aidan." She flashed a pearly-white smile in his direction. "Let me page him for you."

Manicured fingers moved rapidly over an ancient-looking operating system.

"Yes, Sheriff. Do you have a minute to come up front? Aidan MacFie would like a word with you."

They waited in anticipation while the receptionist tried her best to appear busy, thumbing through a stack of paperwork while sneaking peeks at the handsome fireman. Jade imagined he must get quite a bit of attention from female admirers. She wondered if he was currently dating anyone, and then tried to push the idea out of her mind. The last thing she needed was a romantic complication in her life, whatever her dreams might think.

A door opened down the hall. The gray-haired officer's footsteps echoed throughout the building as he approached them.

"Aidan, it's good to see you. I see you brought a friend."

"Good to see you, Sheriff. Wondered if you might have a few minutes to discuss a possible trespassing incident."

"I do."

"Great. I'd like to introduce you to Jade Mackenzie."

"Pleasure to meet you, Miss Mackenzie."

"Thank you, Sheriff Carpenter. Please, call me Jade."

She studied the officer with interest. His deep-set wrinkles gave him the appearance of a seasoned officer. There was a kindness in his eyes when he smiled which immediately put her at ease, even under the unpleasant circumstances.

"Jade found a rather…startling discovery this morning." Aidan said.

"Oh? Well, why don't you follow me back to my office and we can discuss it."

The sheriff led them down a long corridor covered with photographs of officers from years past. Jade's professional eye quickly noticed one antique photo dating to the nineteenth century. The resemblance to Sheriff Carpenter was uncanny. The officer smiled while she studied the image.

"That's my great-grandfather, Sheriff David Carpenter. He traveled the Oregon Trail back in 1849, led a caravan of pioneers from Nebraska to California."

"That's amazing! My great-grandparents also traveled from Nebraska the same year. They settled in Monterey, though my family ended up in San Francisco," Jade exclaimed.

The sheriff nodded with interest. "My great-grandfather settled in San Francisco, but he ended up retiring in Monterey years later."

Jade's eyes widened, making the connection. She searched her memory, realizing her great-grandmother mentioned Sheriff David Carpenter numerous times in her diary.

The seasoned officer opened the door to the last room down the hallway and gestured them inside. A painting of a wagon train and a pioneer family hung on the wall adjacent to his desk. He motioned for Jade and Aidan to take a seat.

"Could I get you a drink, Miss Mackenzie? Maybe a coffee or soda?"

"No, thank you. I'm fine."

"Alright then." Sheriff Carpenter sat behind his desk, folding his large hands beneath his chin.

"What can I help you with today?"

Jade glanced over at Aidan unsure of where to begin.

"So, Jade moved into her family cottage down on Ice Plant Lane a few months ago," Aidan said.

"Oh?" The two men locked eyes with a knowing look.

Jade glanced back and forth between them. "Are you familiar with the area, Sheriff?"

"I am, actually. This may come as a surprise, but our families go way back."

Jade's eyes widened. "Really?"

"You see, my great-grandfather, David Carpenter, was sheriff in San Francisco in the mid-nineteenth century. He eventually retired in the Monterey area. From what I understand, your folks traveled along the Oregon and California Trail the same year my grandfather led the caravan. Our families made a point to keep in touch over the years. When my relatives moved to Pacific Grove, your great-grandparents Cathy and Shane Mackenzie welcomed them with open arms. They'd visit your family's cottage on a regular basis. In fact, quite a few of the families from the original group stayed in contact after settling in San Francisco and Monterey."

"That's unbelievable! I recently came across my great-grandmother, Cathy Brennan's, diary. Her mother married a young Comanche man and moved to his village. Apparently caused quite an uproar with the local town's people when their relationship was discovered, and her parents were killed by the townspeople. She was taken in by two traveling priests who found her in the woods, and they brought her to a nunnery. She was later adopted by an older couple. When her adopted parents died, Cathy left Nebraska and joined a wagon train heading down the Oregon Trail, eventually becoming a natural healer." Jade paused. Cathy Brennan's diary mentioned other things, but she didn't think she should mention them to the sheriff.

"It's full of details about her experiences as a pioneer. She mentioned your great-grandfather several times. Spoke very fondly of him in fact. He helped her out of several dangerous incidents along the trail."

"Thank you. It's incredible that I run into you now," Sheriff Carpenter said.

Aidan folded his hands together and rested them on the mahogany desk.

"Sheriff, some odd things have been happening near Jade's cottage. A cardboard box was left outside her porch sometime last night or early this morning." He motioned towards the package by his feet.

"May I have a look?" Sheriff Carpenter said.

"Please," Jade said with feeling.

"Since you've already opened it, I'd like to take a look before we send it to the forensics lab. I want to get an idea of what we're up against before we get to questioning. I think it will be easier that way."

Jade nodded slowly, thinking that something seemed a little odd about the whole thing, but at least she wasn't being shuffled through red tape.

The sheriff opened his desk and pulled out a pair of rubber gloves before proceeding. Once they were on, he removed the lid. The stench filled the room and he blanched at the putrid smell.

"Oh, boy." After a few minutes of peering at it from different angles and with a flashlight, he put the lid back. He removed his gloves and paged one of his deputies to his office. A tall blond-haired deputy met him at the door and the sheriff gave him instructions to tag the remains for the evidence room. Afterward, Sheriff Carpenter began thumbing through a pile of forms.

"What do you suppose it could be?" Jade asked.

"My guess is that it's most likely a marine mammal, judging by the texture of skin and the smell. Probably seal. There's an accredited biologist in the area that can examine it more closely. Topusana Nocona's her name. I'm sure she'll be able to identify the animal. I'll give her a call. She has an office at the Monterey Aquarium. Would it be alright if I give her your contact information? She may want to inspect the environment by your cottage," Sheriff Carpenter said.

"Of course."

"We're going to start an investigation today. Rest assured we'll find who's responsible for injuring wildlife in the area." The sheriff looked up from his papers, making direct eye contact with Jade. "Miss Mackenzie, I'm going to ask you a few personal questions if you don't mind," he said with a meaningful look toward Aidan.

She nodded, her eyes widening in curiosity.

Aidan looked over. "I can come back later if you'd prefer to discuss this alone."

She smiled at his thoughtfulness. "That's alright, Aidan. I don't mind you staying."

"Absolutely."

The young fireman sat back in his chair with his fingers folded against his chest while the sheriff prepared his examination.

"Jade, when did you move into your grandmother's cottage?"

"It's been over three months ago…back in early June. I've been busy trying to get my antique shop in order since the move."

"Congratulations. We like to support all the small businesses in the area."

"Thank you. I've really been amazed how kind everyone's been in the neighborhood."

"I'm glad to hear that. We're a tight-knit community. It's been that way for as long as I can remember."

Jade nodded, feeling at ease. The sheriff quickly turned to business. "Is there anyone you can think of who might want to harm you?"

She looked up, startled, and began straightening out the hem of her skirt. "Umm…not that I can think of right now. I pretty much keep to myself these days. Work has been taking most of my time. Of course, I'm always meeting new customers at the antique shop. I haven't noticed anyone particularly dangerous. Just the occasional bargain hunter trying to argue down prices."

"Any boyfriends or ex-husbands that might have some unsettled business with you?"

She fidgeted in her chair, aware that both Aidan and the sheriff were waiting for her answer. The fireman looked out the window, sensing her embarrassment.

"Well, I've never been married and have been single for over a year now. The relationship ended amiably, well as much as these things can, I guess." She flushed, looking down at her folded hands.

"Miss Mackenzie, I'm going to ask you to fill out some paperwork, so we have this on file. We can send some officers down to patrol if you feel like you're in danger."

She looked at the sheriff with eyebrows raised. "Oh…. I don't think it's necessary. I'll make sure to keep locked up. I'm sure Morrigan will make a fuss if anyone tries to break in."

"Morrigan?"

"That's her pet raven," Aidan said. "She found the bird outside her cottage and has been caring for it."

The sheriff chuckled, shaking his head. "You don't say? I believe I remember my grandfather mentioning Cathy's pet raven. His mother told a story of a bird named Midnight. He was a kind of mascot at your family's cottage."

"Oh, you're exactly right! Yes, I read about Midnight in my great-grandmother's dairy. It's funny, though: This raven's different than most. She's pearly white. I have never seen anything quite like it."

"That's odd. Perhaps you can mention it to the marine biologist when she gets in touch. Mrs. Nocona's knowledgeable about the wildlife in the area. I imagine she might have information concerning white ravens."

"Oh, I'd love to meet her."

"Alright, young lady," the sheriff set down some paperwork and a pen on the desk in front of her. "Here's a couple forms I'd like you to fill out regarding the incident this morning. Just describe everything you can remember. Are you sure I can't offer you a cup of coffee?"

"As long as it's no trouble." Jade looked up and smiled.

The sheriff grinned back. "Cream and sugar?"

"Oh, sugar would be great. I don't imagine you have any non-dairy creamer?"

"I'll see what I can do. Aidan, can I have a word with you a moment?" Sheriff Carpenter said.

"Sure."

❂

ONCE THEY WERE OUT OF THE ROOM, THE SHERIFF LOOKED OVER HIS friend's shoulder to make sure they were alone. They watched a female patrol officer carry a small box toward the evidence room. She punched in her code, and the door closed behind her with a heavy thud.

"Are you thinking what I'm thinking?" Sheriff Carpenter asked.

"Afraid so. There are just too many coincidences," Aidan said.

"Have you shared any of this with Jade?"

"Not yet. She was pretty shaken up after we spoke. I was afraid I'd upset her even more."

Aidan considered Jade, newly arrived into a danger she knew nothing about. When he was in her cottage, he'd examined the painting Jade claimed to change and felt washed with dread when he studied the man in the shadows. A primal fear, like a forgotten memory, had threatened to surface as he tried to make sense of it all.

"Well, you might want to confide with her once everything settles down. The more she knows, the better. The young lady looks like someone that can keep things to herself. Her family's been entrenched in this community over the years."

Aidan shook his head. "Yes, they definitely sacrificed for this town."

Sheriff Carpenter looked out the window, studying the parking lot filled with police cruisers.

"What about the patrol car I mentioned earlier? It wouldn't be too difficult to send some units to keep an eye on things."

"She seems pretty determined not to have the police involved with security. She really values her privacy. I gave Jade my number last weekend. I'll be checking on her," Aidan said.

The sheriff nodded with a knowing smile.

"Alright, I might send out some extra officers in the area, but we won't station a twenty-four-hour watch if she refuses it. I feel better knowing that you have a handle on things. Could be just kids messing around, but we need to take this seriously."

Aidan glanced toward the room that hid Jade from view. Even so, he could feel the quiet strength and sense of vulnerability he found compelling. Her steel-gray eyes, both nervous and self-assured, made him feel lost and gave him an overwhelming desire to sweep her into his arms and throw caution to the wind. But he knew he didn't dare. Nothing good could come from getting too close, but god...he'd love to try.

But more important, he needed to keep her safe.

He hoped she could manage these testy waters.

⚜

WHILE THE MEN DISCUSSED THE SITUATION, JADE SPENT THE NEXT HALF hour filling forms regarding the morning's incident. After she'd said her goodbyes to the sheriff, Aidan escorted her back to her truck.

"So where to now?" Aidan asked.

"Do you have a shift this afternoon?"

"Yeah, it starts in a couple of hours."

Jade nodded, "I should probably get cleaned up and head over to the shop. Can I give you a ride home?"

"If you have the time, that would be great."

"Of course."

Aidan lived about five miles from her cottage on Ocean Avenue. They drove toward a ten-story building overlooking the Pacific Ocean.

"You live here?" Her eyes widened as she studied the grand architecture.

"I do." He flashed an inviting smile. "Would you like to have a tour?"

53

"Sure."

They parked in the underground garage and then headed to an ornately decorated lobby. A doorman opened a gilded door, gesturing them inside with a welcoming smile.

"Thank you, Donavan."

Jade's mind spun trying to understand how a fireman working for the city of Pacific Grove could afford to live in such luxury.

They entered an elevator adorned in gold and silver wall panels. Jazz played on the speaker system while they rose towards the penthouse suite. The door swooshed open and they accessed the private entrance. They were immediately greeted by a whirlwind of fuzzy black fur. A sturdy Scottish Terrier flopped on his back, his exclamation mark tail thumping the floor.

Jade giggled and went down toward the ground to pet the little dog.

"Oh, you're a darling!"

As the terrier covered her from ear to ankle in kisses, Aidan chuckled,

"That's Dougal," he said, giving the dog a loving pat on the head. The dog licked his owner's hand before curling up on Jade's lap. He placed one paw on her arm, gazing up with his bright, piercing eyes.

"I can see he's taken quite the liking to ye, lass."

"Aww, I love dogs. You're such a handsome boy, Dougal!"

The Scotty's ears shot up while his tongue rolled out in a delighted grin.

Jade giggled and kissed the dog on top of his head. "Looks like he's smiling."

"Appears so."

After petting the pup for several minutes, she stood up, taking in the spacious penthouse. Floor to ceiling windows looked out to the bay, allowing a panoramic view of the ocean and resort.

"Would you care for a cup of coffee?"

"Oh, that would be great."

Jade looked around the room, eyeing antiques dating back to the eighteenth century.

"This is spectacular. Some of these pieces must be priceless."

Velvet backed chairs, mahogany doors, and marble floors provided an old-world charm. She studied a colorful tapestry hanging in the back of the living room. The rural scene was of a medieval Scottish castle surrounded by sandy beaches. A group of seals were congregating near the shore. Several noblemen appeared off to the right overseeing the property while farmers and milk maids tended to their herds and flocks. She was lost in thought studying the exquisite embroidery.

Aidan motioned for her to join him in the state-of-the-art kitchen. He offered his familiar grin while pulling out her chair. She sat down in the breakfast nook, admiring the polished surfaces of his modern dining room. A hush of steam whistled; frothy swirls of the rich expresso blended.

He placed the steaming mug in front of her and smiled.

"Sugar?"

Jade looked up and blinked.

"Yes, thank you."

She reached for the bowl and spooned a teaspoon into her cup. The smell itself was heavenly. The beans were probably something she wouldn't be able to afford for quite some time.

Dougal sat on his haunches gazing up in anticipation.

"I don't think this is for you, good boy," she said.

The pup barked his answer, thumping his stubby tail on the marble floor.

Aidan handed the dog a rawhide stick, which he snapped up immediately and carried to his bed by the bay window.

"He's such a cutie," Jade said. She blew off the cloud of steam swirling above her mug before taking a sip. Her eyes widened as she swallowed. "Oh, this is divine."

"Thank you. The beans are flown in from a private rain forest near Nepal. The owners are friends of mine. The sales fund a non-profit which helps the villagers and creates jobs in the region. It's a beautiful area."

"Wow...I'd love to see it one day." She noticed several framed photographs of various locales. They hung about the room, allowing a glimpse into Aidan's world. She bit down on her lower lip, her brow knitting in wonder.

"I imagine you're wondering how a fireman lives in a penthouse and has the luxury to travel around the world."

"Um...it did cross my mind."

"Figured," he said with a smile. "It's not like firemen are known for raking in the big bucks."

He folded his hands together and let out his breath, before beginning. He took a sip of expresso and sat back in his chair.

"Well, my family came from old money...going way back to the Scotland Highlands. They owned half the countryside according to family sources. Perhaps I'll show you my collection so you can better understand. How does that sound?"

She nodded, excited to begin. "I thought you'd never ask!"

He chuckled and offered his arm. "Shall we?"

"We shall." She smiled, taking his arm.

Aidan gave her a grand tour of his penthouse, going into details about his inherited collection.

Jade nodded with interest while they discussed his rich ancestry and various antiques displayed around the room. She walked over to the back wall to get a better look at the floor-to-ceiling tapestry she'd noticed when they'd entered. It was enclosed by thick glass held together by an ornate golden frame. Her eyes widened when she studied the intricate embroidery. "Is this what I think it is?"

"Depends. What are you imagining, lass?" he asked with a raised eyebrow.

There it was again, she thought. *Back to that Scottish accent. Was he even aware he was doing it?*

"I'm imagining this once belonged to a wealthy noble family, most likely dating around the eighteenth century, maybe earlier. Probably commissioned for a grand event like a wedding or birth of an heir."

He bit down on his bottom lip and the flesh crinkled around his vivid blue eyes. "Good eye. It dates to 1760."

She moved closer to the glass, examining the details. The image was a pastoral scene displaying a medieval castle. Sheep grazed over the lush hills while several peasant women tended to the herd. Well-dressed men in kilts stood off in the distance, surveying the land.

"It's lovely."

"Thank you. The piece has been in the family for generations, passed down from father to son."

"This is remarkable, Aidan. I could spend a lifetime gathering rarities and never find anything that compares with these pieces. Truly remarkable."

<hr/>

THEY SPENT THE NEXT HALF AN HOUR WALKING ABOUT THE PENTHOUSE, examining the many artifacts. Aidan watched Jade's excitement as he told the story of each antique. Her excitement was contagious, and he soon found himself going into detailed histories of his collection. He hoped he could continue piquing her interest, enjoying the way her face lit up whenever she'd come across a new treasure. Her smile was sweet, but her eyes glowed with purpose with every new discovery.

After he'd given his tour, they walked past his bedroom. Jade let out a sigh. She scanned the elegant bedroom set, also dating to the eighteenth century. Grand columns surrounded the mattress and lush bedding, while a reading couch was set up against a bay window overlooking the ocean. For a moment he was lost in thought, imagining her under the covers, wrapped in his arms. A few scenarios flashed though his mind, each more interesting than the last.

She must have had some similar thoughts, because when she finished examining the set, she looked up at him and flushed hotly.

Aidan's tongue darted at the corner of his mouth; a few of of his own ideas surfaced. He'd love to sweep the lass in his arms and lay her down upon his satin sheets. Their eyes met, and the room suddenly seemed quite warm.

"I imagine I'm keeping you from getting ready for work," Jade said.

He bit down on his bottom lip. "Yes. Thank for joining me for coffee. I can't imagine a nicer way to start the day."

"Thank you for helping with my problem. I feel much better."

"Good. I'm glad I could be of service." Aidan held her gaze while he lifted her right hand to his lips, giving the back of her fingers a gentle kiss. He felt her skin ripple as she shuddered, and a warm feeling went through him. Even so, he needed to rein himself in. This wasn't something that should happen, however much he, or they, wanted it to.

He contented himself to holding her hand as they made their way to the elevator.

"Well, lass…you call me if ye need anything."

She let out her breath and looked up into his face, not noticing that her high cheekbones were flushed again.

Interesting. It seemed that Scottish brogue made her heart pound.

"Thank you for showing me your beautiful collection," she said fervently.

He hesitated a moment before pushing the button of the elevator. The door opened with the sound of soft jazz. She stepped inside and wiggled a shy farewell.

After she was gone, Aidan moved to the living room window. He watched the doorman open the large heavy doors for Jade. He admired her long legs that evoked the grace and freedom of a ballerina. She reached for her sunglasses in her purse and smiled.

※

JADE HEADED HOME IN A DAZE. THE MORE TIME SHE SPENT WITH AIDAN, THE more mysterious he seemed. The man was truly an enigma.

She shook her head, trying to focus. After a quick change and shower, she gathered Morrigan and the carrier and headed to the antique shop with a quick glance at the dark phantom in the portrait. Once in the shop, she went to work organizing unopened treasures. The day was busy, the grand opening having worked its magic. There were twice as many customers that afternoon than the previous week. She recognized some faces from the weekend, most likely locals.

She sold several teacups, along with a collection of vintage Depression glasses. Her 49er display continued to bring admirers to the shop. With careful mending, she'd replaced his torn beard and shirt. A man in his thirties took an interest in the gold mining collection. He ended up purchasing one of Mary's western paintings along with Joe Montana's bag of pyrite. The customer explained he was a local high school history teacher hoping to generate some enthusiasm from his class. He figured his students might enjoy learning about goldmining.

Jade smiled while he talked about their lesson plan detailing the Oregon Trail. He jotted down his number on the back of his business card and asked her to call if there were any more historical treasures available. She promised she would.

After she wrapped his purchase, she checked her cell and realized she'd missed three calls from Mary.

Her phone buzzed in her hand and she picked up on the second ring.

"Oh, so glad you answered. I've been trying to reach you," Mary said.

Jade noticed a slight nervousness in her friend's voice. She seemed out of breath.

"Is everything alright?" she asked, her eyebrows knitting in concern.

"Well, yes and no. I did some research on the painting. To be honest, I'm a bit overwhelmed. I talked to Katie last night. There's a local library in

Napa with some old microfiche. She discovered some rather startling information."

"Really? I've had my own strange occurrences going on my end."

"Sounds like we have a lot to talk about. Katie and I moved some things around and can come down this Friday. I know we were just there, but I don't really want to discuss this over the phone. I think you'll understand when we get together."

"I'd love to have you visit this weekend," Jade said.

"Great. We need to start working on the gift basket of wine we won," Mary said.

Jade giggled, shaking her head. "We're definitely going to need some adult beverages to figure this out."

"Yep," Mary agreed with feeling.

"I can make space in the living room if you want to stay at the cottage or just can't find a place in time. There's room on the couch and I can pick up an air mattress on my way home tonight," Jade offered.

"That would be great. I'll give you a call when we know what time we'll be getting in," Mary said.

"Looking forward to seeing you both," Jade said.

She clicked her cellphone off and looked out the store window. A dull ache settled in the pit of her stomach. Despite her anxiety, Jade spent the next hour waiting on customers and cleaning up the shop. She turned the closed sign on the door at five o'clock.

Crimson streaks washed over an amber sky. Jade admired the vibrant sunset as she drove down the highway. Her mind wandered while she headed to Whole Foods to stock up on fresh vegetables, grains, and lentils. She finished loading her grocery cart with a box of cocoa and carton of almond milk before heading to the cashier. Afterward, she stopped at a local department store and picked up an air mattress for the upcoming girls' weekend. After her shopping spree was completed, she headed toward the cottage. With a deep yawn, she drove the foggy road heading toward the ocean. She wanted nothing more than to curl up in front of the fireplace with a good book and a warm beverage. Once she was home, she fed Morrigan and made a simple dinner for herself. After lighting the fireplace, she snuggled on the couch with a steaming mug of hot chocolate. Jade dozed to the gentle sounds of rain hitting the tin room.

Chapter Seven

THE STONE STAIRCASE SPIRALED AT A STARTLING ANGLE. CANDLELIGHT illuminated the dark figures descending the steps. Lightning strikes lit the balistraria, sending jagged beams of light across the castle alcoves. The sound of thunder boomed above when they reached the Great Hall.

A hooded figure took his place at the head of a long, mahogany table. His companions sat down, turning toward their leader in anticipation.

"We have much to discuss. You all know where I stand on the matter. This must be a unanimous decision before we can proceed. Let's begin with Laird Lithgow. What say you?"

"She's a demon, I tell you. MacFie took pity on the creature, but we all know it's heresy. Loneliness is no excuse. She's not of this world. It's an abomination. The creature should be burned at the stake."

An elderly man leaned forward, shaking his head. He stroked the golden crucifix hanging around his long neck. Flickers of candlelight reflected across the precious rubies at its base.

"Her husband's a nobleman. And there's talk that the woman is carrying his bairn. Do yeh ken how much he's given to the church over the years? His family owns most of the deeds of the landholders in the village. For God's sake, man! If our plan were ever found out, we'd burn right along with her."

A cloaked figure made his way forward, his footsteps echoing in the dark. Pale fingers clasped a curved hunting knife which he held toward the circle of men. Firelight flickered off the edges of the blade.

An audible gasp went around the room.

"Once you take its skin...all will be well. We'll burn the atrocity in the flames of holy fire. That will be the end of the soulless one and the spell she has placed on our laird."

He spat onto the concrete floor, while making the sign of the cross. His companions followed suit.

A middle-aged man ran his fingers through his salt and pepper hair. "But their castle's brimming with servants. How yeh suppose we get the vile creature alone?"

"That's where I come in." The group turned toward their youngest member. A youth in his late teens stood from his chair, facing his peers. He scratched the stubble of his auburn beard, licking at his bottom lip. "I can sneak in as one of 'em. Pretend I'm delivering the daily bread. I'll wait until the creature's alone in her garden."

The leader stood from his seat, ready to address his peers. His congregation watched him, eager to hear his decision.

"The soulless one's days are numbered. Her life will be taken on the night of the Hunter's Moon. We will rid our town of both the unholy creature and her unborn bairn. Let us pray."

The scene slowly faded.

A new image began to filter in with sunlight. It shone through a curtain of heavy mist, revealing a medieval castle. A young woman walked barefoot over a bed of emerald moss and pink primroses. She pushed a lock of auburn hair from forehead. Her vibrant blue eyes mirrored the sea surrounding her home. She moved about her garden, straightening the creases of her green-velvet gown while she collected cuttings of rosemary and thyme. She carefully placed each piece inside a dainty wicker basket covered in lavender ribbons.

A white raven perched in the branches of an apple tree, the autumn light spilling over its ivory feathers. The bird watched the young mistress gathering ingredients. When she finished, the bird flew from its perch landing atop her shoulder. She let out a laugh and stroked the raven's head.

"Good, lass. Let's get back home, shall we, my love?"

The image dissolved into a blinding kaleidoscope of color.

Chapter Eight

Jade awoke with sunlight streaming through the lace-covered windows in the living room. She blinked and stretched, surprised she'd fallen asleep on the couch. The fireplace held a few smoldering embers. She rubbed the back of her neck, wincing at a knot that had formed overnight. A heavy wind shook the foundations of the cottage. She moved into the kitchen to set up an antique percolator.

Fragments of the previous night's dream rolled about her head, threatening her peace of mind. She shuddered at the images of cloaked men cloistered away in the darkness.

What did it all mean? Why were they plotting against an innocent woman? The strange men had spoken of her like she was a monster, something unholy. Yet seeing her in the dream, the maiden appeared harmless. It was a lovely image really—a young lady tending to her garden while a blue-eyed raven perched in an apple tree.

She bit her lower lip as the imagery came to mind.

Yes, there was a white raven, not unlike her own. So strange. And had the men mentioned she was with child? Yes, they most certainly did. They wanted to murder the young mother and her "unborn bairn." It was unimaginable…a terrible dream.

She tried to convince herself, yet she knew dreams could have hidden meanings relating to the unconscious. Her grandmother had believed in the powers of dreams, but her mother had disabused that notion. Perhaps Aidan's antique collection set the story in motion. He owned priceless treasures. She couldn't remember anything in his home that reminded her of cloaked men or hidden rooms. She pulled the belt of her robe tight when a shiver ran down her spine.

Jade went about her morning routine in a fog, nearly forgetting Morrigan while she gathered her keys and purse. The raven's plaintive cries called her back right before she closed the front door.

After she'd placed her pet's carrier in the back seat, she climbed behind the wheel, catching her reflection in the rearview mirror. She gasped, seeing the dark shadows beneath her eyes. Her disturbing dreams were beginning to interfere with her daily life. Jade tried her best to push the terrible images from her mind. She blared the truck's radio, singing along to Pink's latest hit. Before long, she was standing in front of Antiquities and Novelties of Pacific Grove, ready for another day of selling.

The morning started off well, several repeat customers arrived to examine her latest merchandise. She spent the day organizing newly arrived items and assisting her clients. The afternoon went slowly, so she decided to close early and try to regain her peace of mind.

The rest of the week crawled by, and it was with great anticipation when Friday finally arrived. The jingle of the bell announced Mary and Katie's arrival. A strong wind blew autumn leaves across the stone floors. Jade hurried over, wrapping her arms around her friends' shoulders.

"I'm so happy to see you! There's supposed to be a terrible storm passing through this evening. I set up the pullout couch and a new air mattress with plenty of quilts and blankets if you'd like to spend the night," Jade said.

Mary nodded. "Perfect. We'll follow you over."

"I was thinking about stopping by my favorite Chinese restaurant along the way. We could bring some to-go boxes home with us."

"Sounds great. I've been craving Chinese food," Katie said.

The women took separate cars, moving slowly in the dense fog. Their windows were covered with drizzle by the time they arrived at the restaurant. They found two parking spots near the front door of The Golden Dragon Restaurant. Jade's friends exchanged glances before entering. The modest building was decked out with early Christmas lights and vintage Coca-Cola signs. A pile of shingles littered the walkway. The neon sign above the door flashed intermittently. Mary and Jade's eyes widened as they followed their friend inside.

"Trust me. You're going to love it," Jade said.

The sky darkened and a strong gust knocked several more shingles onto the walkway. They hurried through the door to escape the chilly air and falling debris. The family-run restaurant was busy that evening. Every table was full while a crowd of hungry customers waited inside the packed lobby. The rich scents of ginger and lemongrass permeated the room, making the friends' mouths water.

Jade handed Mary and Katie to-go menus. A petite elderly woman with a shock of white hair smiled behind the glass counter while an orange waving cat figurine swayed silently.

"Jade, it's good to see you."

"Lovely to see you, Quiyue. Your dishes will go perfectly with a stormy evening."

"Oh, yes. We have two fresh pots of hot and sour soup ready in the back. One is vegetarian just like you enjoy."

"Perfect! We'll definitely order a couple of those to go."

The sound of thunder rumbled overhead while they placed their orders of steamed rice, family style bean curd, hot and sour soup, and onion pancakes.

Twenty minutes later, Quiyue returned to the lobby with their takeout orders. The women thanked the owner and carried their dinner outside, bracing against the fierce wind. Jade turned on the heater in the truck and headed to the cottage, Mary and Katie following close behind. The soft chattering of Morrigan echoed from the backseat. Light sprinkles turned to hail by the time the women arrived home.

As Jade parked outside, whitecaps pummeled the shore. The friends carried their overnight bags, dinner, and Morrigan to the front door, bracing against the heavy wind and rain. Sheets of water sluiced downward, and Jade ushered everyone inside the cottage.

"Wow! That's some crazy weather. So glad you invited us to stay over," Katie said.

"Seriously. I'm glad we don't have to drive anymore tonight," Mary said.

Katie nodded, wiping raindrops from her face with the back of her hand.

"It's pretty spooky out there. Ladies, make yourselves comfortable while I make a fire. There's a good chance we will lose power in this storm. I'm going to change into pajamas afterward. It's been a long day and the cottage can get a bit drafty," Jade said.

She showed them the coat closet and told them to go ahead and put their belongings anywhere they would fit. While her friends changed and put away their things, Jade busied herself at the fireplace.

⚜

MARY GRINNED, EMERGING FROM THE BATHROOM WEARING PINK FLANNEL pajamas and bunny slippers. "We're going to have an old-fashioned slumber party. Love it!"

Katie went in next. Several minute later, she reappeared in forest green silk pajamas and matching ballet slippers.

Once the fire started, Jade headed to her bedroom to change into a Victorian-style nightgown with lace sleeves and pearl buttons down the front.

Mary whistled. "Looking good, Miss Mackenzie!"

Jade giggled, heading towards the kitchen. She turned on the radio to her favorite hip-hop station.

"Let's get this party started!"

She waved her friends over to the dining table and began filling three crystal glasses with a bottle of Chardonnay from their victory basket.

"We're all going to need some liquid courage for this," Jade said.

Mary and Katie exchanged puzzled glances. "Jade, we haven't even told you what we found," Katie said hesitantly.

Outside the thunder roared while rain pounded down onto the tin roof. Jade took a sip of wine then set her glass down on the table.

"I know, but Mary doesn't joke about this kind of thing. Besides...you really need to see this."

They followed her to the fireplace, their eyes widening at the sight of the portrait.

"What do you think?" Jade said.

"I can't believe it. This has to be a joke," Mary said.

"It's not. I really wish it was."

Katie stepped closer. "The figure of the man is much closer to the shore...and there's an object by his feet." She squinted and stepped closer to the mantel. "Almost looks like an animal skin."

65

"That's what I see, too," Mary said.

Jade released her breath. "I'm so glad you're here. That you can see it. I've been feeling like I'm losing my mind."

Jade filled the women in about discovering the box of mangled seal flesh on her porch. Her friends shook their heads in astonishment. Their eyes widened when she described her visit to the sheriff's office. When she was finished, Mary and Katie sat down cross-legged in front of the fireplace staring up at the portrait. Jade refreshed their glasses before taking a seat on the air mattress. The fire crackled in the hearth, casting shadows across the floor. They were quiet for several minutes, listening to the rain beat down onto the tin roof.

Katie pushed back her auburn curls from her forehead and sighed. "This is all so incredible."

Mary stood up and headed over to her briefcase by the front door. "And Jade, girl, you don't know the half of it."

Jade's brow rose while her friends sorted through a stack of paperwork and reference books, organizing them neatly on the dining room table. Katie plugged in her laptop and scrolled across her keyboard. "Oh, good. I found it," she said, leaning toward the screen.

"We've been doing research," Mary said. "I was curious about the portrait's artist. I found several similar scenes, but it's the subject matter in them that's disturbing."

While Mary and Katie organized their findings, Jade warmed their Chinese food in the microwave and served up the rice and tofu in blue and white ceramic plates. She poured hot and sour soup in matching bowls.

"Let's have dinner before we get started. I get the feeling I might not have an appetite once I hear what this is all about," Jade said.

"Good idea," Katie said.

"That smells delicious. I didn't realize how hungry I was," Mary said, eyeing the triangles of fried tofu covered in steaming garlic sauce as she finished tidying up the stacks.

The women helped themselves to supper, quietly focusing on their meal. Jade fidgeted with the chopsticks, absently poking at a bright green hunk of steamed broccoli that remained on her plate as she waited for Mary and Katie to finish eating.

Katie was the first to break the silence. "Have you ever heard of the term *selkie*?"

"Selkie?" Jade asked.

"Yes, the term originated in Celtic mythology. They're also mentioned in ancient tales pertaining to Iceland and some remote areas in Europe. The stories mimic mermaid legends to some extent, but there's some significant differences between the two." Katie pushed her plate to the side, folded her hands and leaned forward. "Selkies are mythological creatures able to change forms—seal to human. They shed their skins in order to live on land."

"Sounds like *The Little Mermaid*," Jade said.

"Not exactly, but there are some similarities. These tales are recounted in many Scottish legends and folklore."

Mary took a sip of Chardonnay and reached for her stack of papers. "So, we've both been doing our own research and have come up with some differing versions of the legends. Many of the stories report unusual relationships with human beings...romantic couplings. One of the common versions revolves around a man stealing a female selkie skin and hiding it. This allows power over the woman, often forcing her to cohabitate with the man, bear him children, be a good wife, etcetera."

Jade looked back and forth between her friends, trying to absorb what they were saying.

"This is all very interesting. I love a good folk story, but I'm not sure I follow where this is going?"

The women exchanged glances. Mary stood up and walked over to the fireplace. She pointed toward the figure in the painting. "I've been searching through books and other resources pertaining to both style and form relating to this work. One theme came up again and again. Katie and I both believe the portrait to be selkie related. The dark form by the man's feet appears to be a seal pelt."

Katie turned her screen towards Jade. "I found versions from various sites. It's difficult to determine if the man is the selkie or the skin belongs to a selkie woman."

"Oh my god, this is all impossible," Jade said. "A few days ago, I visited Aidan at his penthouse and..."

"Penthouse?" Mary exclaimed, her eyes bright.

"We stopped by after our visit to Sheriff Carpenter's office. I was pretty shaken up after the discovery of the animal skin outside my house."

"Aidan lives in a penthouse?" Katie interrupted.

"I know, right? Not what you'd think from a fireman's salary. Well, he inherited quite a fortune from his Scottish ancestors. I discovered an eighteenth-century tapestry in the living room. It's priceless. And this is funny since we're talking about seals and selkies. The focal point of the tapestry focuses on a wealthy estate by the sea. It reminded me of my dream I had the other night."

"Dream?" Katie took a sip of her wine and leaned forward.

Jade sat back in her chair and took a deep breath. "All right, please keep an open mind. I'll understand if you think I've lost it."

The women exchanged puzzled looks.

"Just take your time, Jade. We want to understand what's going on," Mary said soothingly.

Katie nodded.

"Alright," Jade said. She searched her friends' faces, mustering her courage to continue.

"A few nights ago, I had the most bizarre dream. I found myself inside an ancient Scottish castle. Candles were everywhere. I remember a group of men climbing a spiral staircase. I couldn't see their faces at first. They were concealed by black hoods, but I could hear them chanting as they climbed. I'm not completely sure, but I believe they were speaking in Latin."

"Interesting," Katie said. She folded her hands under her chin and leaned forward.

"The leader wore a golden cross, but he did not seem holy in the least. The men gathered around a long table in a Great Hall. They were discussing the fate of a laird and his wife."

"A laird," Mary said. "Like a Scottish lord?"

"Yes," Jade said. She rubbed her temples as the memories surfaced.

Mary put her hand on her shoulder. "Are you okay?"

"Yes. It's just the dream was so disturbing. The things they were discussing…it's unimaginable."

"Take your time," Mary said.

"Well, they started by talking about a laird and his lady. They referred to her as 'it'. She was an abomination in their eyes. The men seemed to belong to a bizarre religious cult. They discussed plans of stealing an animal skin, then murdering the wife. But the dream changed, and I was suddenly in a castle watching a beautiful red-headed woman collecting herbs. There was a white raven nearby."

Katie and Mary exchanged glances, leaning forward in their chairs.

"The woman was completely oblivious of the danger. I wanted to warn her somehow, but all I could do was watch the scene unfold."

"Dreams can be doorways," Katie said. She placed her hand over Jade's hand. "I've had my share of odd occurrences."

"I would love to hear more about that," Mary said. "I've sensed you've been holding back for some time now."

Katie smiled at her friend. "I promise to fill you in on everything some time. Let's focus on Jade's dreams for now."

Mary nodded. "All right, but I'm holding you to it. I'm dying to hear what's been happening in Napa."

"We'll need another bottle of wine for that story."

The women laughed while the wind whipped against the windows. Katie pushed back a lock of auburn curls from her forehead. "Who's to say it's just your imagination, Jade? I believe dreams can be a connection to the past and future. Don't you find it strange that Aidan's tapestry seems connected to the painting above your fireplace? Do you suppose he might know more than he's admitting to?"

"I'm not sure, but there were a couple odd things I noticed in the sheriff's office. Aidan and Sheriff Carpenter kept exchanging strange looks. I got the feeling they knew more than they were letting on."

Mary took a sip of wine. "Might be time to have another chat with your fireman friend."

Jade bit down on her bottom lip. "Yeah, I think you're right."

Katie took out her notebook and a pen. "Would you describe the tapestry again? I want to see if I can find any similar works."

"Aidan said it dated to the mid-eighteenth century. There's a castle on the right side with an expansive sea off to the left. Both villagers and noblemen appear in the scene. Peasants work the fields while the noblemen survey the property. There were several large seals along the beach. I was impressed by the details. The tapestry is well-preserved."

Katie's fingers moved over her laptop keyboard, pulling up images relating to selkie legends of Europe. "This is the article I mentioned earlier. So, selkies, also known as Selkie Folk, are half seal, half human. Legends describe the creatures leaving the sea in order to transform. They must shed their seal skin to live on land. The stories suggest that some of the female selkies would marry human men. Their offspring were known to be heroic sailors and even sea captains. This article traces selkies to the MacFie Clan in Scotland. Apparently, their ancestry began centuries ago when a high-born chief took a female selkie for his bride."

"Seriously?" Jade startled.

"What's wrong?" Katie asked

"MacFie? That's Aidan's last name. The fireman."

The women exchanged wide-eyed glances.

"This is beyond crazy." Jade cupped her fingers behind her neck and paced back and forth in front of the fireplace. "Every time I think I can make sense of these things another bizarre coincidence is thrown into the mix. How do I even rationalize this? It's exhausting."

Mary picked up Jade's wine glass and carried it over to her friend.

"It's going to be all right. You're not alone. We're in this together and I'm sure we can figure this out. Take a deep breath, drink your Chardonnay, and let's do some more research. The more answers we have, the less daunting this will all seem."

Jade smiled. "You sure know how to make a girl feel better. I'm so grateful you're here."

Katie grinned. "We're happy to help. And Mary's right. Knowledge is power. Let's just keep researching until we find the answers."

Jade joined her friends at the table and filled their glasses.

"Alright. You ladies ready for an all-nighter?"

"Absolutely," Mary and Katie chimed in unison.

They spent the next several hours online, researching articles, comparing notes, and finishing the last bottle of wine from their trivia gift basket. Around midnight, Jade stood up from her laptop. "You girls need to read this article I just found."

"Oh?" Mary said.

"Apparently, there's a group that formed back in Scotland in the early eighteenth century. They were Christian fanatics. The article suggests they went after selkies in the same way witches were hunted during the Salem Trials. Unlike the public persecution in Massachusetts, the interrogations were conducted under the cover of darkness. Both women and girls went missing. There seems to be great wealth associated with this group. Secret benefactors supplied the funding for their cause, and with their money and influence, the cult was rumored to victimize families of noble birth."

A feeling of cold lead settled in the pit of Jade's stomach. Her mind flashed to the tapestry and the strange dream of the woman in the garden.

It all had to be a crazy coincidence. Or was it?

"That's odd," Katie said. "Let's keep looking for answers." They stayed up another three hours exploring related articles. It was four in the morning before they reluctantly headed to bed, their minds racing with fantasia, facts, and figures relating to selkies, sea nymphs, and all things aquatically paranormal. The sound of their breathing blended with the scratching outside the cottage walls.

Chapter Nine

Jade was awake before her friends the next morning. Morrigan did not understand the concept of sleeping in—she started cawing for her breakfast at seven o'clock. After the feeding, she made a pot of strong coffee and sat out on the porch watching the sunrise. The heavy rains had lifted, revealing a sparkling clear morning. She dozed on the porch swing despite the caffeine dose. The next time she opened her eyes it was noontime. Jade headed back inside to make brunch. While she busied herself cutting up fresh vegetables and stirring them into a tofu scramble, her friends began waking up. She mixed a handful of fresh spinach and mushrooms and stirred the mixture into a sizzling frying pan.

"Oh, boy," Mary rubbed her temples and groaned. "Does anyone have any Ibuprofen? I don't think I've drunk so much since my college days."

Katie nodded. "I do. I also have some fresh feverfew leaves in my bag if you want to munch on them. They're crazy bitter, but really help with a bad headache."

"That would be perfect," Mary said.

The women took their seats and helped themselves to coffee and breakfast. A knock on the front door made them wince and turn. Morrigan cawed in answer. Jade rose from her seat, pulling a robe over her Victorian night dress. She smiled when she realized Aidan was standing outside with a handful of energy bars.

"Good afternoon." His grin faded as the other women waved to him from the kitchen table. "Oh, I'm sorry. Didn't realize you had company." Aidan glanced over Jade's shoulder and waved. He offered a boyish smile when he noticed her Victorian nightgown. "Thought you might like to join me on a run. I usually do mine in the morning but had a late shift."

Jade smiled. "Of course. Would you like some breakfast, I just made a tofu scramble?"

She gestured him inside, pointing to the table.

"I'd love to, but I usually eat after my workouts."

"Ladies, this is Aidan," Jade said, ignoring Mary and Katie's exchanged look. "He stopped by to see if anyone is willing to join him for a run. Are you girls up for joining?" Jade asked.

"Normally, I would," Katie said. "But my head has other plans today."

"Looks like you ladies had quite the night," Aidan said, blue eyes widening as he took in the crystal glasses and empty wine bottles strewn around the room.

Jade bit the corner of her lip, glancing away. "We had an interesting time."

Aidan studied her face as if waiting for more.

"I'll go change into my running shoes. Be right back!"

She hurried to her bedroom while her friends struck up a conversation with Aidan. A few minutes later she returned wearing pink cutoff shorts and a matching top. He smiled, openly admiring her toned legs and figure. Jade grabbed her water bottle and filled it in the kitchen while Aidan waited patiently.

"Are you sure you don't want to join us?" Jade offered again.

Mary and Katie leaned back in their chairs at the kitchen table.

"Nope. I'm pretty tired from last night," Mary said.

Katie nodded in agreement. "You two go and enjoy yourselves."

"Alright, see you in a while then," Jade said.

Aidan held the door for her, and they stepped outside into the amber light.

They raced down toward the shore with the breeze blowing through their hair. The rain had stopped, but the wind was frigid.

Despite her drinking escapades, she felt invigorated. Jade increased her strides as they neared the shoreline. Aidan rose to the challenge, keeping with her pace.

"Did you have a good night with your friends?"

"Yes, we've been doing some research."

"Research?"

"Yup. It appears we may have some clues relating to the subject matter of my mysterious portrait."

"Oh?" His carefree smile slowly faded.

"Have you ever heard of a selkie?"

Aidan's face paled and he slowed his pace to a stop at the waterline.

Jade stopped alongside him. They locked eyes, bracing themselves against the strong gusts.

"I can't help but to feel you've been holding back information, Aidan. Especially concerning the package on my doorstep. You don't really have the poker face you think you do."

His eyes widened, surprised by her directness.

"Both you and Sheriff Carpenter appear to be hiding something. I didn't want to pry into your family background, but now it seems to have something to do with what's been happening at my cottage."

She folded her arms over her chest, her gray eyes glowing with purpose. He stepped closer and took her hand in his. "That's fair. You're right for wanting answers. Before I tell you everything though, you need to prepare yourself. Once you hear what I have to say, there's no going back. It will change the way you see the world. Ignorance is bliss. Please consider this seriously before I go on."

Jade rested her hands on her hips and took a deep breath.

"I need to know what's happening to my home, Aidan."

His fingers laced through hers and he led her toward the tidepools. They were quiet, listening to the pounding of the surf. *How quickly things changed since their first run together*. She took a seat on the back of a log, stretching her legs out toward the sea.

Aidan paced for several minutes, clearly trying to collect his thoughts.

"I told you that my family came from old money," he said finally, "back in the Highland Hills of Scotland."

"Yes."

"The story of my ancestors is a complicated one. Much of their history is mixed up with folklore and speculation. For years, I believed the more fantastical tales to be nothing more than urban legends. They were simply stories to entertain the younger generations. That belief changed when I was a senior in high school."

Jade looked up, noticing the pain in his eyes. He sat down next to her on the log, gazing out at the tides.

"My great-grandmother, Edina MacFie, left Scotland in the late eighteenth century. They moved to the Americas, eventually making Virginia their home. Edina left a written record of her life in a collection of leather-bound books. I discovered the diaries when I was a teenager."

Jade nodded with interest, surprised by their connection.

"So, I should let you know I had a wonderful childhood. Being the only child, my parents equally invested in giving me a life filled with love, support, and financial stability. We traveled every summer, went camping whenever we had the chance. My mother and father were so in love, and they made a point of carving out alone time. In fact, they enjoyed sharing a special date night every Thursday." He bit down on his bottom lip and ran his hand through his wavy hair.

"It was autumn of my senior year of high school. My parents were out on one of their weekly dinner dates. There was a particularly strong storm that evening. The power went out around seven o'clock. Luckily, I had a flashlight ready. Figured I do some reading to pass the time but couldn't find anything interesting. So, I went up to the attic to poke around. I can still remember how peaceful it was listening to the rain hitting the roof, sorting through boxes, and storage bins. It seemed like hours had gone by, looking at photo albums, discovering old comic books, and childhood treasures. I was about to head back down when I noticed a hope chest pushed beneath a card table. I'd never seen it before. I dusted it off and pried open the lock. There were a couple of vintage gowns and articles of clothing on the top layer. Buried beneath the wardrobe, I discovered a collection of old diaries. I couldn't believe my luck. It was like finding a hidden treasure. The first book was tarnished with age, yellowed woven paper covered in beautiful flowing handwriting." Aidan's voice was soft as he spoke, almost wistful.

"As I read the pages, my flashlight battery started to die, so I lit some candles and began thumbing through the diary.

"My eyes widened when I read the date of the first excerpt. It read, May 2nd, 1760.

"I soon discovered the diary belonged to my great-grandmother. She talked about her love for the sea, meeting my great-grandfather, and missing her family. At first there were everyday passages—daily happenings at the homestead, her different gardening projects. Edina was a healer and expert on herbal remedies. She created tinctures and teas whenever there was an outbreak of the flu in the castle. One passage even explained how one concoction saved the life of her servant maid during childbirth."

Jade's eyes widened. "So strange. She sounds like my great-grandmother, Cathy Brennan. She was also a natural healer."

Aidan nodded her head. "That is interesting. I remember you mentioned reading your great-grandmother's diary. Sounds like an incredible woman. Well, my ancestor's healing practices eventually caught notice of some of the more religious residents of the town. Some even suggested she was practicing witchcraft. She spoke in great details about a group of zealots that had taken an unhealthy interest in her family. But here is when her story becomes truly bizarre. She mentioned that these men could never know her true nature. She believed herself to be a creature known as a selkie."

"Are you serious, Aidan?"

"Yes. This will make more sense when I tell you the second half, Jade," Aidan warned.

"All right. But even with everything you've said, I don't see how that could happen," Jade answered, attempting a lighthearted tone to belie her growing apprehension.

"So, I read for hours. My great-grandmother went into great details describing her history with the Selkie Folk—a semi-human race from the sea. Their stories are similar to mermaid tales in some ways, but they are more closely related to seals. Some of her people, she explained, sought out a life with humans, shedding their seal skins and joining their mates on land. Male selkies would often find lonely wives and widows to cohabitate with. Some female selkies were forced to live among humans. Men found ways of stealing their skins while the females were onshore. Hiding their pelts forced the women to stay on land."

"Oh my god. Like the skin left outside my door?" Jade said.

"Well, yes and no. There may be a connection. The sheriff and I are working on it."

"He knows about this?"

"He does. I think you'll understand why when I explain the rest of my story." Aidan studied the cresting waves hitting the shore.

"Folklore suggests selkies occasionally visited the shores of Scotland," he continued. "In order to spend time on land, they'd need to shed their skin. There are many tales of female selkies being lured into relationships by humans. The common example is a man discovering a female selkie nude on the beach and stealing her sealskin, thus forcing her to lay with him or marry. These forced relationships could last for years, even resulting in hybrid offspring. Yet the reluctant bride would continuously long for the sea. If the selkie eventually recovered her pelt, she would return to the ocean permanently. This was heartbreaking for the children left behind, not understanding the true nature of their mother."

"Are you telling me your great-grandfather stole the skin of a selkie and made her his wife?" She shook her head in astonishment.

"I know this sounds bizarre, Jade. But maybe when you hear the rest you'll understand," Aidan said.

"I'm listening."

"My great-grandmother, Edina, explained a handsome laird discovered her asleep by the shore. When she woke, she couldn't find her sealskin. Over time, they fell deeply in love and married. My great-grandfather did not steal anyone's pelt. It was her choice."

Jade nodded. "Well, that's good to know, but are you really suggesting your great-grandmother was nonhuman?"

Aidan pushed his fingers through his hair and closed his eyes. "I know how it sounds, darlin'. Please just bear with me awhile longer."

Jade nodded and placed her hand on his arm. "Sorry, I'm listening."

"Thank you. There were many passages in her diary describing their whirlwind romance. She spoke of her excitement of having his bairn and the plans they had made for their future, but the diary passages eventually told a darker tale. My grandmother mentioned a secret cult called The Hunters. They referred to themselves as priests, but they were not good men. Their religion took elements of Christianity mixed with blood rituals and dark magic. Their practices were ruthless. The cult's main objective was to wipe out the Selkie Folk and kill every one of their offspring. They wanted desperately to destroy Edina and her entire family. The fact she was pregnant made them desperate. You see, their greatest fears were being played out before their eyes. The idea that Selkie Folk could procreate with humans, and produce hybrids, was an abomination in their eyes. So, they set a plan in motion to destroy the MacFie legacy. They began by trying to turn the town's people against my great-grandmother. They suggested she was a witch, using dark spells and potions to further her craft. They brought their concerns to the magistrate, but it went no further. Her reputation was solid. She'd helped so many families with her remedies, many came forward to speak in her defense. So, her case never went to trial.

"After they failed to tarnish her reputation, they took a more direct approach. A few of their followers infiltrated the MacFie castle. At dusk, one of the cult members discovered her alone in the garden. While he was attempting to stab her in the belly, my great-grandfather arrived and wrestled her attacker to the ground. He killed the intruder but was fatally wounded in the process. Edina cradled his head in her lap as he said his final farewell, begging her to flee toward the safety of the underground tunnels. By the time she escaped, the entire castle was ablaze. Another cult member set fire to the Great Room. The servants scattered from the castle in droves." Aidan's voice deepened with anger and resolve, his accent unknowingly getting stronger with his passion.

"Once she'd escaped, my great-grandmother went by foot to her brother-in-law's estate. He was quiet while she explained everything that transpired. Heartbroken by the loss of his brother, he vowed to find the perpetrators. Fearing for his sister-in-law's safety and her unborn child, he arranged safe passage to America. My great-uncle secured for her both a residence and financial security on one of his Virginia estates. He promised to re-build his brother's home, hoping she might return one day with his brother's heir.

"My great-grandmother arrived safely but suffered greatly during her journey. She ended up giving birth two days after she arrived in Virginia. She had a healthy baby boy, my grandfather."

Aidan's face grew pale and he stared out toward the sea. "I was just getting ready to open another journal when my parents discovered me up in the attic. I peppered them with questions, demanded they explain everything. They tried their best to brush it off, suggesting my great-grandmother had an over imagination bordering on mental illness.

"I could see the worry in my father's eyes. I wanted desperately to find out more, but he refused to talk about it. The following Thursday, I went back to the attic to finish reading the diaries. The boxes were nowhere to be found.

"When my parents arrived home that evening, I asked where they'd taken the diaries. Seeing I wasn't going to quit until I received answers, they promised to explain everything if I'd just give them a little more time. My mother kissed me on the cheek that night before bed while my father stood in the doorway. I remember his eyes—blue, just like mine—were so full of pain. She asked me to be patient, and I'd understand everything soon enough. I told her I'd hold her to that promise." Aidan let out his breath and shook his head.

"It wasn't long after when my parents received news that my great-aunt was ill. They decided to visit her in Scotland. They wanted to bring me with them, but I was finishing senior projects. So, they said their goodbyes, promising me they'd answer all my questions once they returned home.

"But they never had the chance. Their plane crashed west of the Highland Hills." He looked away, choking back tears.

Jade reached for his hand. "Oh, Aidan. I'm so sorry."

He gave her hand a squeeze and nodded. "I know ye understand what it's like, lass. It's a terrible thing losing your parents."

He turned toward the shore, his eyes glistening with tears.

"I was devasted of course, just a few months away from graduation. Not only had I lost my family, I suffered terrible guilt for arguing with them before they left. Days turned into weeks and my sorrow turned to anger. I began acting out in class and ended up getting a week of detention. I decided to take my mind off things by getting a fake ID and sneaking into local pubs and bars. I drank myself nearly unconscious. One night, I had the misfortune of getting a beer bottle smacked over the back of my head. Must have passed out because I woke inside the drunk tank the next morning. Sheriff Carpenter bailed me out. You see, he'd been a family friend for years. After a long talk, I agreed to stay with him and his wife until after graduation. His family took me under his wing, even helped find a good attorney to sort out the legal details of my parents' will. It turned out they left everything to me. I was stunned to learn not only did I inherit a substantial amount of money and the family estate, but I was also deeded our ancestral home in Scotland. It turned out that my aunt's castle was jointly owned with my father. Sadly, my great-aunt soon passed after my parents' deaths. The shock of losing both her brother and sister-in-law while battling cancer proved too much."

"I'm so sorry, Aidan."

He nodded. "She was a dear woman. The property deed is solely in my name now. There's a full staff that continues to manage the estate."

"The castle belongs entirely to you?"

He nodded. "It's quite lovely. The castle overlooks the sea, and the hillsides are covered in heather and wildflowers in the spring."

Jade's eyes widened with understanding. "Is the tapestry in your penthouse…"

He smiled. "Yes, that's my ancestral home. The same one my great-grandmother spoke of in her diaries. Her brother-in-law was true to his word. He fulfilled his promise by successfully rebuilding the castle. Some say it's as grand a building as it was back in the eighteenth century. Some of the old furnishings and artworks were saved during the fire. It's a beautiful place to visit, but my home has always been in the States. After graduation, I enrolled in the Fire Academy. Once I'd graduated, Sheriff Carpenter asked to speak with me privately. He figured I was old enough to learn the truth."

Jade put her hand on Aidan's arm. "There's more?"

"Afraid so. It turned out that my parents shared my great-grandmother's diaries with both him and his wife. They believed their family might still be in danger considering their dark history with the Hunters."

Aidan brushed the back of his hand against Jade's cheek. "Lass, this is going to be a shock to you, but our family histories overlap."

"How so?"

"You already know that Sheriff Carpenter and your great-grandparents crossed the Oregon Trail together."

Jade nodded. "Yes, he mentioned it to me the day at his office."

"Yes, what he didn't mention was the fact my ancestors eventually settled into the Monterey area about twenty years after yours."

She looked up in surprise.

"Sheriff Carpenter suggested your relatives knew my family. You see, the Hunters eventually tracked down my relatives in Virginia, so they were forced to move again. My family made the Monterey Coast their home in the nineteenth century. The MacFie and the Mackenzie families had met in Scotland years before. My relatives apparently found your family again and worked with them in the cattle business in Monterey. The sheriff and I are still trying to find out more details, but we think it could be connected to what's been happening at your cottage.

Jade stood up, dusting sand from her shorts. "I don't even know what to think, Aidan. This is all so incredible. You're suggesting our families were not only friends, but allies against a dangerous religious cult? I had no idea we were so connected. Do you really believe your ancestors' heritage to be traced to a non-human race called the Selkie Folk? Things like that aren't real! And I'd never even heard of your family or the Carpenters before in my life until I came here!"

He paused, biting his lower lip. "I know what the legends say. The British Isles have many tales and folklore pertaining to a half-fish Merpeople. Stories of the Selkie Folk originated in Ireland, Scotland, and the Orkney Islands. They were told to be seal-shapeshifters able to shed their skins and live amongst humans on land. My father's family trace their roots back to the Clan patriarch and a selkie maiden."

"So, I've heard," Jade said.

Aidan's eyes widened. "What do you mean you've heard?"

"My friends and I were researching my painting last night. The subject of selkies came up in conversation, relating to similar portraits. Your family name appeared online."

Aidan reached for Jade's hands.

"You asked me if I believe in selkies, and I'm not quite sure how to answer. One thing I do know for certain is there's been a threat against my family for centuries. I'm afraid our ancestor's connection has brought trouble to your doorstep."

"Do you think the package was left by a member of this cult...The Hunters?"

Aidan's brow knit. "It might be a warning of some type due to our family's connection. I don't know if their aim was to get my attention. If that was what they wanted, they were successful."

Jade rubbed her temples, trying to understand everything she's heard. It was all crazy, and yet, the coincidences were undeniable. "Look, Aidan, I'm sorry, but this doesn't make any sense."

"Your reaction is exactly why I was hesitant to mention this before, Jade. I didn't want to worry you." Aidan threw his hands into the air and began pacing.

"Worry me? It's a little too late for that! For god's sake, I have a portrait in my cottage changing before my eyes. I can't get through the night without having nightmares. And let's not forget the awful animal skin left on my porch. I just spent an entire evening researching selkie legends and now you're suggesting they can be real."

Aidan's mouth fell open. "You mentioned your research earlier, but I still don't understand. I thought you said you were having a girls' night?"

"Well, yes and no. We did some research concerning the portrait. It led to our findings of selkie myths. I told them about the seal pelt and my bizarre dreams."

"What do your friends think about all of this?"

"They're open-minded to all of it. We just want answers."

"I'm sorry, Jade. I've been trying to find a gentle way to explain this, but I didn't want to overwhelm you. And it looks like that's exactly what I did. You're white as a sheet."

"It's just so much."

She glanced up into his aqua-blue eyes, reading his pain and hesitation. *Was there something more he was holding back?* she wondered. Jade was quiet for several moments trying to put together all the pieces.

"Are you sure that's everything?" She searched his face, trying to determine what he was thinking.

Aidan reached down, stroking the side of her face with the back of his hand. "I promise to tell you everything. Please just give me a little more time."

Her eyes widened in surprise. *There's more?*

Before she could question him further, his lips found hers. There was an urgency in his kiss that wasn't there before. Aidan gathered her in his arms. He slipped her shapely legs over his lap, his fingers moving through her sandy-blond tresses. For a moment, time stood still.

Cries echoed down the beach. The couple turned in surprise when Mary, Katie, and an unfamiliar woman approached. They exchanged embarrassed glances, realizing they interrupted a private moment. The stranger was in her mid-thirties, with long black hair and ebony eyes. She wore khaki slacks and an orange windbreaker.

"Sorry to interrupt. I'm Dr. Topusana Nocona...the marine biologist for the Monterey Aquarium."

"Oh, yes, the sheriff told me you might be stopping by," Jade said breathlessly.

"I was in the area and tried to call, but your phone went straight to voice message. I normally like to make an appointment first, but I had some important information concerning the package left outside your cottage," Topusana said.

Jade let out her breath, glancing between the biologist and Aidan. "It's getting pretty windy. Maybe we should go back to the cottage to talk."

Chapter Ten

JADE LED THE GROUP BACK TO HER COTTAGE. HURRYING INSIDE TO ESCAPE the wind, the door slammed shut behind them.

"It's freezing this afternoon. Would you all like some coffee?" Jade asked.

"That would be wonderful," Dr. Topusana Nocona said.

"I'll go and make a fresh pot. Please make yourself comfortable." She gestured toward the dining room table. Morrigan cawed from the bedroom then flew to her mistresses' shoulder. The biologist's eyes widened when she noticed the bird.

"Sheriff Carpenter mentioned your white raven," Topusana said.

"Yes, she flew into my life when I moved in. Landed in front of my door with an injured wing."

"Your bird is extremely rare."

"I'd thought as much. I'd love to learn more about them so I can care for her properly until she's ready to leave. Do you have any information you'd be willing to share?" Jade asked.

Topusana nodded, following Jade into the kitchen. "Well, for one, the white raven is not albino like many believe. In albinism, there is the absence of melanin pigmentation, which is what gives most albinos their red or pink eyes. The condition is called leucism which is only a partial loss of color or pigment. This isn't the case with white ravens. You see how Morrigan's eyes are pale blue?"

Jade nodded with interest.

"White ravens are normally cream-colored, but yours is nearly true white. Interesting," Dr. Topusana mused. "Do you mind if I take a photo? I've never seen one quite like her before."

"Please, do," Jade said.

"Thank you." Dr. Topusana snapped a few photos on her phone. "Have you decided to keep her as a pet or set her free?" she asked.

"Well, I've been trying to figure it out. I want Morrigan to have a full life and am not sure if she'd be happy inside," Jade said.

"You should know that a normal lifespan can be anywhere from 10-30 years. I grew up on a reservation in Nebraska. My great-aunt discovered an injured black raven on her fortieth birthday. I was just a toddler when it happened. She nursed the bird back to health and the two became inseparable. The raven follows her everywhere. My aunt turned seventy last month and the bird continues to be her constant companion."

"Really? That's amazing."

"Yes, so if you decide to keep her, it could be a long-term commitment," Topusana said.

"That wouldn't be a problem. I believe pets should always have a forever home," Jade said.

The biologist nodded. "That's good. May I examine her?"

"Please."

Dr. Nocona reached her arm toward the raven and said, *"Tuhcorpiauku."*

Jade's eyebrows raised in question. Morrigan landed on her wrist, locking eyes with bright curiosity.

Topusana smiled while stroking Morrigan's snowy white feathers. *"Tuhcorpiauku* is the Comanche word for raven."

"Oh, that's a lovely-sounding word!" Jade exclaimed in admiration. "Are you Comanche? I have some Comanche heritage and there is so much I would love to learn," Jade said.

"Oh?" Dr. Topusana stepped closer, her dark eyes brimming with curiosity.

"Yes, my great-grandmother Cathy was half Comanche and half Scotch/Irish. She was a remarkable woman. Her parents perished during a village massacre. She herself barely escaped with her life. She eventually joined the Oregon Trail and found clues about her family legacy that had brought about her parents' deaths and eventually became a natural healer and visionary. According to her diary, she dreamed of her birth parents during her trek out west. Her memories of her mother aided her in finding cures and remedies for her traveling companions. Some of her dreams and visions predicted upcoming tragedies along the trail." Jade brushed a locket of gold hair from her eyes. "It's funny since I've been having strange dreams myself. I had a really odd one right before the package was left outside my door…" She trailed off, suddenly aware of Dr. Topusana's intense gaze. "I'm sorry, probably sounds a bit strange." Jade said.

"I don't find it strange at all. Although I'm a scientist, I believe some mysteries in life are unexplainable. I have family members with the same kind of visionary gift you spoke of pertaining to your great-grandmother. It's considered a blessing in our culture." Dr. Topusana smiled warmly. "If you're curious about learning more about your Comanche heritage, I'd be happy to help."

"Thank you. I have so many questions. My mother and grandmother collected Native American artifacts, which is a big part of my interest in antiques. They passed down a lovely collection of Comanche dolls from the early nineteenth century. Been wanting to find a nice display case for them. I've been so busy with the shop I haven't found the time. But I'm grateful to have them. I just wish I had asked more questions when my mother or grandmother were alive. My mom always expressed a desire to explore our family tree. Reading my great-grandmother's diary has left me with more questions than answers," Jade said.

The marine biologist nodded. "I think we never fully understand ourselves until we understand the journey of our ancestors. There is a generational legacy that connects past and present. I would be more than happy to help you research. Maybe we can get together and talk about it over coffee?" Topusana offered.

"Oh, I would love that!" Jade said

"Great. I'm looking forward to it. I'll leave you my card before I leave, and we can get together."

Morrigan stretched her pearly wings over the biologist's shoulder, then flew back to her perch.

Dr. Topusana smiled, watching the white raven preen her pearly feathers. "You've taken wonderful care of her, I can see. The wing is fully mended.

If you decide to keep Morrigan, you'll want to reach out to the wildlife department. You need a license to own a raven in California," Topusana said.

"Good to know. I was wondering what the rules were regarding ravens as pets," Jade said.

"I think you'll be able to keep her if you want. I know some employees at the California Wildlife Center who can help you. I'd be happy to put in a good word. It's obvious you've taken great care of Morrigan."

"Oh, I'd really appreciate it! I've grown so fond of her."

"It shows," Topusana said. "I think she'd have a lovely life with you at the cottage. And I'm sure she'd love to fly around the beach if you'd feel comfortable giving her a bit of freedom."

"Absolutely," Jade said. "She can have all of the freedom she desires."

Morrigan flapped her ivory wings and flew back to her perch.

"Well, I came to let you know my findings concerning the animal skin."

Jade carried a tray of mugs with hot coffee to the dining room table along with a pitcher of chilled almond milk.

Everyone took their drinks, while Topusana laid out brochures relating to the local wildlife.

"I brought some pamphlets from both the Monterey Aquarium and Pacific Grove Natural History Museum. I think the extra literature might help explain why this case is particularly unusual," Topusana said.

"You have no idea," Jade said, glancing at Aidan.

The marine biologist opened one of the brochures and pointed to a glossy image of seals.

"Harbor seals, sea lions, and occasionally elephant seals are common in the Monterey region," Topusana said. "The area is rich with marine life. When I received notice from the sheriff concerning the animal remains, I figured I'd probably be examining a Harbor Seal from his description."

"What did you uncover during the necropsy?" Aidan asked. He bit down on his lower lip awaiting her answer.

"Well, when I examined the flesh, it was surprisingly well-preserved. They'd kept it on ice at the police department, since I was out of town when I received the call. I expected to see a significant amount of decomposition, possible maggots, or at least fly eggs."

Mary grimaced. "Eww, that sounds disgusting."

Topusana smiled. "It's all part of being a biologist. You get used to those kinds of things. On my initial examination, the flesh presented as recently butchered. The skin was fresh."

"But there were maggots on the skin when Aidan and I opened the box. And the smell was putrid," Jade protested.

"Interesting. The skin was clean upon examination. I had to double check with the sheriff concerning the collection time and processing."

"Strange," Katie said.

Topusana nodded. "Just wait, it gets stranger. After taking some tissue samples and comparing notes, I ruled out the possibility of it belonging to a Harbor or Elephant seal. And it's definitely not an otter by the size of the hide."

"So, what is it?" Jade said.

Topusana sat up in her chair, surveying the group. Everyone waited in anticipation of her findings.

"The flesh matched the DNA of a Grey Seal."

"Why is that so strange?" Mary asked.

"Grey seals are Atlantic sea mammals. You'll find them in areas like Great Britain and Scotland," Topusana said.

"Scotland?" Jade's eyebrows raised while she locked eyes with Aidan.

"So, I don't want to bog you down with too many facts but let me give you a quick description. The Grey Seal, the *Halichoerus grypus*, is found on both shores of the North Atlantic Ocean. They're often referred to as 'true seals,' or earless seals. Grey seals are often over six feet long. They also have longer noses compared to their North American relatives.

"The fact the DNA matches a species that's not native to the area is surprising enough. Another troubling finding has to do with the condition of the skin. This animal was surgically dissected."

"Dissected?" Jade echoed in horror, covering her mouth with her hand.

"I'm afraid so," Topusana said. "Someone expertly removed the back flippers of the animal. All five digits were accounted for and fully webbed. The back flippers spread out like a fan in a living seal, allowing them to move along the water. Someone used what appeared to be a scalpel on the flesh. Whoever did this must have knowledge concerning medical procedures. This wasn't the work of a teenager or some random prankster. The back flipper was surgically removed."

Aidan sucked in his breath, shaking his head in anger.

"That's horrible," Mary said. She pushed a brunette curl behind her ear. "Who would do such a thing?"

The group was quiet for several moments while they considered the new information.

"This mystery deepens by the day," Jade said.

Mary shook her head. "It really does."

Topusana sat up in her chair. "I wish I could offer you more information. I've never seen anything like this on the Central Coast."

She reached into her purse and handed everyone her card.

"Please, if you have any more questions, feel free to call. I have an office at the Monterey Aquarium. It's best if you phone ahead if I'm away doing field work." She jotted a number and name on the back of the card before handing it to Jade. "You can call the California Wildlife Center anytime you're ready to register your raven. Make sure to mention our meeting. There shouldn't be a problem getting a license for Morrigan."

"Thank you," Jade said. "I really appreciate you coming down on your day off. I'll make sure to contact the Wildlife Center tomorrow morning."

"I'm happy to have helped. Please call anytime if you have any more questions or concerns," Topusana said.

"I'll definitely do that," Jade said. She walked the biologist to the door, and everyone said their goodbyes.

After the marine biologist left, Jade joined her friends at the kitchen table.

She turned to Aidan, locking eyes with him. "Do you feel comfortable speaking about our earlier discussion?"

He nodded. "I think I better if we're going to get to the bottom of all of this."

Jade went back to the kitchen and prepared another pot of coffee. She refilled everyone's mugs before sitting down. The women turned toward the young fireman in anticipation.

"Just to warn you, it's a lot to take in," Aidan said.

Katie smiled and nodded. "Take your time. Why don't you just start at the beginning. This is a no judgement zone."

Mary nodded. "Absolutely. The more information we have, the better."

"Alright then. Here goes..."

For the next hour, Aidan related the tale of his ancestral home, his great-grandmother's diaries, the Hunters, and his parents' death. The women were quiet while he spoke. Afterward, he waited for their response, looking as unsure of himself as he had with Jade on the beach.

Katie was the first to speak. "I appreciate your candor and honesty, Aidan. I'm so sorry for your loss. It can't be easy reliving such painful memories. We have a lot to figure out and the more information we have, the better."

Mary nodded. "We really do appreciate everything you've told us. This mystery is deepening every day. I'm most concerned for Jade's safety. What if these men come back? And what if they don't stop with special deliveries, but attempt to break in?"

Aidan hesitated before speaking. "Sheriff Carpenter agreed to arrange extra patrol cars around the neighborhood. There's also been nightly home checks since the visit to his office." He looked down at the floor trying to avoid Jade's glower.

Jade folded her arms. "I thought we'd agreed to no patrol officers. We discussed it in Sheriff Carpenter's office. I really wished you'd told me about this!" Her face flushed as she felt her temper rising. "I really don't appreciate being watched. Why did you keep this from me?"

"Would you have agreed to it if I had, lass?" he challenged, looking up.

"Probably not, but it's my decision to make!"

"You're a stubborn one."

Jade gasped in anger and stormed out the front door.

It was only a couple of minutes before she heard the door open behind her. She didn't turn, keeping her seat on the porch swing and staring at the foggy beach.

"Your friends sent me out. They said that it was an invasion of your privacy to have arranged private security. I should have discussed it with you, but Jade...I'm just worried about you. You need protection. You didn't have the information about my family's history."

She nodded silently. The wind whipped her blond curls across her face and she absently pushed them away, marring the fresh tear tracks on her face in the process. "And who's fault is that? This is all craziness! First, I have people sneaking around my cottage leaving seal pelts. I have a painting which keeps changing before my eyes, a mutilated seal that becomes fresher with time on my doorstep, and someone I really care about has been lying to me! Am I just supposed to smile and take it on the chin? It's too much!"

The tears spilled over her flushed cheeks and she turned toward the shore. Aidan put his hands around her shoulders and gently pulled her against his chest. Angry as she was, she melted willingly into his arms.

All the bottled-up pain and frustration from the past year bubbled to the surface. Unable to keep it all in, Jade wept. She cried for the death of her mother and grandmother. Their absence left a hole in her life. Tears rolled down her rosy cheeks as she began to let it out, confessing her doubts and fears of running a business by herself. Living alone was one thing, but the frightening occurrences at the cottage made her doubt her sanity. Aidan was silent while she spoke, gently stroking her golden tresses.

When she was finished, he reached into his pocket and handed her a handkerchief. Her eyes widened spotting his family crest embroidered on the soft cotton.

She took it gratefully.

"Are you always so prepared?"

"I try." He winked, offering his lop-sided smile. "It's also a handy spare smoke mask if someone needs help."

"This is so embarrassing," she said, wiping away the tears. "You probably think I've gone off the deep end." She shook her head trying to regain her composure.

"No, Jade. You're human. I think you're incredibly brave, living out here by yourself, running a business, and dealing with something completely unnatural. You'd be crazy if you weren't afraid and frustrated. I'm just sorry to have caused you pain."

She shook her head. "No, Aidan. It's not your fault. I'm the one that should be sorry. I just took out my frustration on you. Can you forgive me?"

"That depends. Do you really care about me?"

Jade gazed into his dazzling blue eyes. His lips found hers and he pulled her into a tight embrace. Being in his arms was like nothing she'd ever experienced before. Every touch was a new sensation. When she leaned back, his mouth followed the curve of her neck to the top of her blouse. His fingers followed, gently sweeping down her middle, then over her hips, pulling her closer. Her body ached for his touch. After several moments of pure bliss, Aidan gazed down at her face, kissed her forehead, and took her hands in his.

In a husky voice, he whispered. "I'm going to suggest an idea. Please take a moment before answering."

She looked up into his piercing eyes, feeling like she could look at them forever. Jade bit her lower lip waiting.

"I don't want to sound presumptuous, but I have an idea." Aidan said.

"Oh?" Did he want her as badly as she wanted him? *Just say the word*, she thought.

"What do you think about me staying at the cottage?"

Jade blinked and her mouth fell open in disbelief.

"The couch is fine, of course," he said quickly. "I'll stay out of your way. Many of my shifts are forty-eight to thirty-six-hour ones, so I won't be here around the clock." He hesitated a moment before adding, "I just think it might be safer having an extra pair of eyes."

Jade took a deep breath, her mind racing.

"You want to stay at the cottage with me?"

"Just for safety reasons." Aidan smiled innocently, but Jade noticed a flicker of mischief in his eyes.

"You really think I'm in that much danger?" Her heart pounded and her thoughts were going a mile a minute. *This day kept getting stranger by the minute.*

"I wouldn't ask you if I didn't think you were. I'd like to believe this is all a bizarre coincidence, but I'm not willing to gamble with your safety. Of course, if you'd rather, you are welcome to stay with me. I'd be more than happy to set you up in my spare room. I just figured you'd say no."

"You're right. I would have. I'm not allowing anyone to scare me out of my home. It's all I have left of my family."

"I understand that."

"I'll need to think about this," she said.

"You don't have to answer right away. Just consider it."

Jade released her breath, placing fingertips against her temples. She could feel the beginning of a headache and hoped it wouldn't develop into one of her dreaded migraines. She was both intrigued and terrified of the idea of Aidan staying at the cottage. Yet, she was fiercely protective of her privacy.

Katie and Mary stepped onto the porch with their overnight bags. "We're planning on heading back while traffic is light. Are you going to be alright, Jade? I hate to leave you alone with this mess. My staff is limited this week with college midterms. A lot of my part-timers are students. If you'd like some company, I could swing by on Saturday. We could do a little more research, maybe get to the bottom of this mess," Mary said.

"Thank you. I'd love to have you visit next weekend. But only if you're sure you can spare the time away from the gallery," Jade said. "Two weeks in a row already seems like it could pressure you."

Mary nodded. "Shouldn't be a problem. I think most of their exams will be over by then."

Katie sighed, glancing between her friends. "I wish I could stay longer, but my fiancé and I are taking a trip in a couple of days. Daniel wants to show me the wedding hall in Kinvara, Ireland. We have a few more details to iron out before the big day." She pushed back a lock of auburn hair from her forehead, studying Jade's face with concern.

"Of course. You've both helped me more than you'll ever know. I understand you need to head back. Aidan's been kind enough to offer to keep me company while you're gone."

The women exchanged amused looks and nodded.

"That's wonderful to hear. Please take care of our friend," Mary said. She smiled when Aidan placed his arm around Jade's waist.

"It will be my pleasure," he said with a wide grin.

Katie studied the couple and grinned. "I think you're in good hands, Jade."

"Yes, I agree," Mary said.

Aidan helped the women carry their bags to Mary's car.

Mary and Katie waved goodbye while they drove down the cobblestone path. Jade bit down on her lower lip, wrestling with Aidan's proposal. After a few minutes of hesitation, she glanced up into his hopeful eyes.

"All right," Jade said.

"All right?"

"I'd like you to stay. To tell you the truth, I've been spooked terribly this past week. I just want to make sure you'll be comfortable. My cottage is nothing like your fancy penthouse."

He chuckled and reached for her small hands. "I'll be fine. Believe me."

"What about Dougal?"

"Yes, I thought about it. I can board him at the Pacific Grove Pet Hotel. He's stayed before and they took good care of him."

"Why don't you bring him with us? He'll miss you."

"Are you sure? What if he frightens Morrigan?"

"Let's give it a try and see how they do. I can close her off in my bedroom if there's any issues."

"I'd love to bring him. He's very well house trained and no longer chews everything in sight like he did when he was a puppy," Aidan said.

"Well that's good to hear. He's so adorable. I'm looking forward to having you both." She glanced up at Aidan's handsome face, wondering what she'd just gotten herself into.

"Do you have to work tonight?"

"Nope. I'm off until Wednesday afternoon," he said.

"Great. I don't need to be at the shop until tomorrow morning. Would you like to pick some things up from your place?"

"Good idea. I'll pack some clothes and dog supplies. Dougal will be happy to have a little adventure. He has a dogwalker when I'm at work, but he gets lonely at the penthouse by himself. I think he'll enjoy the extra company."

Jade glanced at Aidan. He had readily offered himself for protection, so she was sure that he wouldn't take advantage of the situation. After all, it was her home turf. Still the thought of him sleeping in her home gave her a few ideas.

He caught her eye and grinned. She blushed at having been caught. It was entirely possible that he had some ideas of his own.

Chapter Eleven

JADE GATHERED HER PURSE AND KEYS BEFORE DRIVING AIDAN TO HIS penthouse. Autumn leaves blew across the oak-lined streets of the quiet neighborhood. Pumpkins and gourds adorned many of the surrounding homes. Her mind wandered. With everything transpiring the past few weeks, there hadn't been time to display her prized collection of vintage Halloween decorations. Maybe she'd decorate this week. It would be a nice distraction.

Donavan met them at the front entrance, greeting them with a blur of ebony fur and offering his familiar welcome once they left the elevator. The terrier thumped his tail on the marble floor, sitting on his haunches at Jade's feet.

She reached down and scratched him between his ears while his tongue rolled out in excitement.

"I think he prefers you over me," Aidan said. He grinned while shaking his head. "I'll be back in a few minutes. Just need to pack some clothes and get the pup's food and bowls together."

After petting the dog, Jade strolled through the penthouse. It was still as memorable as the last time she'd visited. She was studying the MacFie tapestry again when Aidan came up behind her with a duffle bag and Dougal's bed and supplies.

"Can I help you carry something?" Jade asked.

"If you could just walk Dougal to my car, it would be of great help." The dog was running in circles at the sight of his leash.

"Sit, Dougal," Aidan said sternly.

The terrier immediately sat for his master. After he'd placed his harness and tether, Aidan gave the dog a pat on his head and handed him over to Jade. "He's all yours."

"Thank you."

She followed Aidan into the elevator and pressed the gold button.

Donavan's eyes widened when the couple arrived in the lobby.

He held the door and smiled.

"Have a good day, Donavon."

"Thank you, sir. Good day to you and Miss Mackenzie."

Aidan loaded his Ford Explorer and followed Jade back to the cottage. Once inside, they were greeted by Morrigan's welcoming caws. The terrier's ears perked up as he watched the bird landing on Jade's shoulder. Surprisingly, he wagged his tail and went off to explore his new surroundings.

"He's such a good boy," Jade said. The raven cocked her head, studying the new roommate with curiosity.

"I'm surprised he's being so well-behaved," Aidan said. "He barks whenever he sees other dogs and completely loses his mind around cats. He's never seen birds this close before, but I guess birds are okay in his book."

"I'm happy they like each other. Here, let me show you around," Jade said.

She took him to the coat closet near the front door. "You're welcome to hang your clothes in here. There's plenty of room."

"Thank you." He set his tote bag inside, planning to unpack later.

"Why don't you set up Dougal's items in the kitchen?" She pointed toward an empty cupboard by the sink. "There's room for his food and goodies."

"Great," Aidan said. He stationed his dog's bag of kibble, treats, and wet food inside.

"Feel free to drop his bed anywhere you'd think he'd like. There's space by the refrigerator for his food and water bowls."

Aidan filled a bowl with kibble while Jade poured water into his dish. They put his bed by the fireplace and continued the tour. When they passed the bedroom, Aidan turned his head slightly and Jade felt the heat rising to her cheeks while they walked by. The four-poster antique bed had plenty of room.

"The bathroom's over here," Jade said.

"That's a nice clawfoot tub," Aidan said. He glanced toward the candles and smiled. "You like to treat yourself?"

Jade blushed again, imagining Aidan using her tub with the candlelight playing over his sculpted physique. She thought she heard Aidan's breath hitch, but she continued the tour trying to ignore her thoughts. They ended up back in the kitchen after the tour.

"Feel free to use the cabinets and fridge for groceries. There's plates and cups," she said, pointing toward the shelf next to the sink.

"Looks like we might be getting a storm." Aidan said, nodding out the window to the darkening clouds.

"It does. Oh, just so you know, I use the fireplace most nights. I lose my power quite a bit. There's also a flashlight and candles in the drawer by the sink."

"Perfect."

"Would you like me to start a fire?" Aidan asked.

"Oh, thank you. The matches are over there," she said, pointing above the mantel.

As he kneeled toward the hearth, she admired his muscular form. Having him stay at the cottage would be pleasant in many ways. After Aidan set the fire, he walked over to the kitchen counter. Shadows lengthened while Jade prepared dinner.

"Can I help?"

"I appreciate the offer, but you should get settled in first. I know you haven't had time to change after your run this morning. I pretty much interrupted your whole day," Jade said apologetically.

"I'm grateful you did. I wouldn't want you to go through this alone, Jade."

She smiled. "I'm glad you're here. It's a comfort for sure. Go get yourself comfortable. There's fresh towels in the bathroom next to the sink."

"Thank you. A shower sounds great."

Jade busied herself setting up dinner. After a few minutes, she heard the water running down the hall. She tried to focus on cooking, but her mind kept drifting to Aidan. She pictured his powerful body in her clawfoot tub, the jet spray rolling down his hard muscles and tight abs. Her breath hitched while her mind wandered. She smiled to herself, imagining his look of surprise if she dared to step over the porcelain tub, cloth in hand. He'd turn to face her, pulling her firmly against his eager body. She sighed, allowing the fantasy to unfold.

She was chopping zucchini into serrated slices when Aidan walked up beside her, planting a kiss on her rosy cheek. He smelled of lavender soap and light cologne. She breathed in his clean scent and smiled.

"Would you like some help?"

"Yes, thank you. Would you care for a glass of wine?" Jade asked.

"Sure."

"Red or white?" she asked, proffering bottles of Cabernet and Chardonnay.

"Cab would be great. Thank you."

He uncorked the bottle. She filled their wine glasses while thunder boomed overhead.

Aidan raised his glass for a toast. "To new beginnings."

"New beginnings," she said.

They locked eyes and took their first sip.

"I can manage the frying pan if you want to take a shower, lass."

"That sounds like a lovely idea, thank you."

She took her glass of wine to her bedroom. After picking out a comfortable pair of lounge pants and button-up nightshirt, Jade headed to the bathroom. She undressed looking at the steamed-over mirror. Knowing Aidan's nude body had been in her shower only moments before was arousing. She let out a sigh, allowing the hot jets to ease her tense muscles. Her fantasies were creative when it came to the handsome fireman. She wondered if he felt the same.

Once she dried off and dressed, she made her way back to the kitchen. He glanced at her flushed cheeks and damp curls. He gave her a wink, and then took a sip of his wine. They worked in comfortable silence while they finished chopping fresh vegetables for the stir-fry, breathing in the rich aroma of garlic and onions. The meal was nearly finished when Dougal began barking beneath the fireplace mantel.

Jade rushed into the living room, imagining he was bothering Morrigan. The bird, however, was on the other side of the cottage nestled on her perch. The terrier was on his haunches, growling aggressively at the portrait.

"Oh my god!" Jade cried.

"Dougal, that's enough," Aidan said sharply.

"No, it's not his barking! Look at the painting!"

The man in the portrait was knee deep in the ocean.

"It's impossible. The figure was on the shore this morning. Now, he's submerged," Jade said.

"Yes, I remember."

Jade looked up at Aidan, trembling. "You do see it?"

He reached for her hand, entwining his fingers around hers.

"I definitely see it. You're not imagining things."

"Thank god. I don't understand how this could happen. It's impossible, right?"

"You're not crazy, love."

Her eyes filled with tears of gratitude. "I'm really glad you're here, Aidan. I don't think I could do this alone."

He embraced her gently, kissing the top of her head and she melted against him.

"Let's have a seat by the fire and enjoy our wine. We'll figure it out."

She nodded and followed him to the couch. He deposited her there, turned off the stove, and sat down next to her on the couch.

The logs crackled and popped, sending tiny sparks into the air. The wind howled, shaking the beams of the cottage. They listened to the waves crashing along the shore, gathering strength in the approaching storm. The lights flickered for several moments then went out altogether.

"Oh, not again. Every time there's a storm the power goes off," Jade complained.

Aidan put his arm around her slender shoulder and leaned in for another kiss. She lost herself in his embrace, no longer concerned about the power outage.

Firelight reflected in his vibrant blue eyes. "Well, I can think of worst things than cuddling up by a fire with a beautiful lass and a nice bottle of Cabernet."

She snuggled against his chest, releasing her breath.

"This is pretty nice," she said.

Aidan's fingers combed through Jade's golden curls. She was lost in his embrace as gentle kisses became more urgent. His tongue swept across hers while he pulled her body closer. With the back of his hand, he followed the curve of her neck, his touch sending an explosion of sensations throughout her body. She shuddered while he took his time, eventually trailing down the small of her back. He was clearly more experienced than she was, *not that that's hard,* came the thought, but she was eager to let him show her what he could do. He gathered her in his powerful arms, gently lowering her onto the couch. He considered her flushed face as his hand grazed over her cheek. With expert care, he reached beneath her top, releasing the back of her bra clasp. Trembling with anticipation, she felt his fingers freeing the buttons of her nightshirt. Jade's breath hitched as his tongue followed the outline of her breasts causing a warm glitter of reflected firelight to trail over her skin. His warm breath sent goosebumps running over her body. Sighing beneath his toned chest, her fingernails splayed through his dark waves, his manhood awakened. His eyes met hers, asking the question without words.

She whispered, "Yes."

His eyes glimmered with desire while he eased her lounge pants to the floor. Aidan smiled down, kissing her softly on the lips. She waited with bated breath when a knocking at the front door made her jump. Dougal raced toward the sound, barking and scratching at the wooden barrier.

Jade glance up at Aidan in bewilderment.

"Stay here, darlin'."

She nodded, large eyes glimmering in the firelight.

He moved to the door. "Who's there?"

"It's Sheriff Carpenter."

"Oh, just a second." He turned to Jade with an apologetic shrug. Her face flushed while she fastened her bra and put her clothes back in place, nodding to Aidan when she was ready. He smiled, giving her a wink. Opening the door, he gestured for the officer to come inside.

"Sorry to disturb you."

"Not a problem, Sheriff."

"Let me light some more candles," Jade said.

Sheriff Carpenter glanced at Aidan with raised brows.

"It's all right, I filled her in about everything."

"Very good. So, Aidan told you about the patrol unit we've stationed by the cottage?"

"Yes."

"There's been some more findings, I'm afraid."

Jade looked back and forth between the two men.

"Why don't you have a seat at the kitchen table," Jade said.

"Thank you." He took a seat, placing a small paper bag in front of him. Jade's eyes widened with curiosity.

"Could I get you a drink, Sheriff?"

He looked down at the table, noticing the half empty bottle of wine.

"No, thank you. I'm on duty."

Jade nodded, opening a kitchen drawer. She found two candles and brought them out to the dining room table. As the wax melted, the aroma of cinnamon filled the cottage.

"We've been sending units out every night. And of course, Aidan's been keeping an extra eye on the place," Sheriff Carpenter said.

"Yes, I wasn't thrilled about finding out about the patrol units, but I've accepted it."

"I'm happy to hear that. I think you might change your mind about the extra security when you hear about our recent findings," Sheriff Carpenter said.

Jade glanced over at Aidan with her brows knit, then turned back to the sheriff. "What's happened?"

The officer leaned forward with his hands folded. "Well, things have been uneventful the past few days. However, the case took a strange turn this evening. A few hours ago, two of my deputies spotted a group gathering down the beach about half a mile past the cottage. They'd started a bonfire but were having difficulty with the wind and drizzle. Appeared to be four of them. The suspects were wearing black robes with their faces covered. Once they noticed the patrol cars, they left in a hurry. By the time the officers made it down the hill, they'd scattered. The search is still active."

"So, there were men in black robes having a bonfire on my property?" Jade shivered thinking back to her dream.

Sheriff Carpenter nodded, his eyebrows pulling together. "I'm afraid there's more, Miss Mackenzie." Aidan reached for Jade's hand.

"The suspects left some disturbing items behind. We believe them to be occult in nature. A collection of items was stacked next to the bonfire—fragments of bone, clumps of hair, and a crystal bottle filled with clear liquid. It appeared to be an altar of some kind. The objects were saturated by a red substance. We're having samples tested at the lab and we don't want to assume that it's blood, although it seems possible. The officers also mentioned there was a terrible odor drifting from the burning pyre.

Once they put out the fire, they noticed something strange. Seemed like an animal carcass had been used underneath the bonfire. They discovered a pelt, mostly charred, but there were pieces of bone and sinew left behind. If I were to guess, it was another seal carcass."

Jade shook her head and closed her eyes. "Oh my god. That's horrible."

"Yes, I agree. The deputies made some other disturbing discoveries during the investigation. I need to show you something, young lady. Please, try not to be frightened. We'll get to the bottom of this investigation."

She glanced up at Aidan and he squeezed her fingers.

"What is it, Sheriff?"

He reached for the bag on the table in front of him. A flash of silver reflected the soft candlelight. Jade's eyes widened at the sight of the antique.

"Where did you find that? It's my great-grandmother's brush. I always keep it in my bedroom by my vanity!"

"The deputies found it near the fire. My deputy reported one of the suspects dropped the brush when he fled. Your property's been dusted for fingerprints, so we're able to return it to you. The discovery is concerning. I don't want to jump to conclusions until we have all the facts, but we can't rule out the fact that human hair is used in ritualistic practices."

"Hair?" Jade asked with fear, touching her head.

"Afraid so. They could have been using it for spell casting or whatnot. We had a similar case a couple of years ago. The perpetrators were never caught."

"If they were in possession of my brush, they must have been in my house!"

Aidan clenched his jaw. "Your cottage isn't safe. What if they come back when I'm not here?"

The thought was terrifying, but she was adamant. "I'm not letting these men terrorize me out of my home."

Aidan threw his hands in the air and began pacing in front of the fireplace.

"Lass, you are *rag-mhuinealach!*"

"Pardon?"

"You are the most stubborn woman I've ever met. What's it going to take? Imagine if one of these men breaks into your cottage when you're alone? My god, lass! Don't ye ken? It could mean your life!"

Jade crossed her arms and turned her back.

She was infuriated by his demands. *Why did he break out into a Scottish accent every time he was excited?* It would have been funny if not for the serious circumstances.

"I'm not leaving."

Aidan glanced over at the sheriff and shook his head.

"Miss Mackenzie, I would advise you to get a security system if you insist on staying. This really isn't a safe situation. We'll station more patrol cars, but it's not a twenty-four-hour watch. I wish it could be, but there've been cuts to the police department this year. We'll do what we can. It really would be best if you stayed somewhere else until we figure this out."

"I appreciate your concern, Sheriff, but I'm not leaving my home. I promise to call an alarm company first thing tomorrow. I'll use the same security system I have for my shop. And I'm sure the dog will bark if anyone comes close to the house."

Aidan's sighed looking defeated. Jade placed her hand on his arm. "I'll bring Dougal to the store when you're not home. Just in case. I don't want anything happening to him," she said.

"I appreciate it. Just wish you'd worry about your own safety."

"I understand. But please understand, this is *mine*."

Sherriff Carpenter stood up from his chair.

"I'll be in touch, Miss Mackenzie. Please call the station if anything else comes up. We'll keep an eye out. Let us know if you change your mind about staying somewhere else."

"Thank you, Sheriff."

The couple watched the officer make his way outside, briskly moving down the cobblestone path as sheets of rain blurred his vision. They were both quiet after he'd left. Jade was emotionally exhausted; a romantic evening having turned into something unexpected.

She sighed. "Would you like some dinner?"

Aidan let out his breath and nodded. "Thank you."

She refreshed their glasses of wine before heading to the kitchen. She brought out bowls of rice and vegetable stir-fry to the dining room table.

They ate in silence, trying to figure out their next move.

"You're a mighty fine cook, Jade."

"Thank you. Appreciate your help tonight."

He nodded. "My pleasure."

The conversation dragged while they worked through their supper. An uneasy tension remained throughout the meal. The sound of thunder rumbled in the distance. Jade barely touched her meal, imagining faceless men rummaging through her bedroom. The thought chilled her to the bone. Aidan brought the plates to the kitchen, insisting on washing the dishes.

"Thank you. I'll set up the couch with your blankets and pillows. Make yourself comfortable," Jade said.

He nodded, balancing their dinner plates in his arms. After she'd finished, Jade peeked into the kitchen.

"Your bed's set up for you. Hope you have a goodnight."

"Appreciate it. Goodnight, Jade."

She watched Aidan snap a leash on Dougal for his evening potty break. When they were outside, she headed to her bedroom with a heavy heart. As she readied herself for bed, her mind raced, trying desperately to take in everything that had transpired that day. It was impossible to fall asleep, so she tossed and turned beneath her quilts, eventually falling into a dreamless slumber.

Chapter Twelve

THE NEXT MORNING, JADE WOKE EARLY TO THE SOUND OF MORRIGAN'S cawing for breakfast. She slipped on her robe and slippers and padded toward the kitchen. When she made her way past the living room, her eyes fell on Aidan, fast asleep on the couch. The blankets had slipped from his bare chest, revealing perfect washboard abs. He looked so peaceful sleeping in his boxer shorts, unaware of her admiring gaze. Her eyes wandered over his powerful legs, and then widened at the sight of his feet. Jade stepped closer for a better look. She blinked, noticing a slight webbing of excess skin filling the space between each toe. The deformity did not take away from his stunning physique, however. In fact, it made him unique in her eyes. He was the most handsome man she'd ever seen. Perfect in every way. She sighed, shaking her head. She imagined the abnormality to be a birth defect and quickly looked away, not wanting to invade his privacy. As she headed to the kitchen, Morrigan flew to his perch, eager for her first meal of the day. Dougal left his bed to join them, thumping his tail on the hardwood floor.

"Alright, boy." She filled his bowl with kibble, topping it off with a scoop of wet food.

Dougal immediately set to work licking his bowl clean.

Jade concentrated on preparing breakfast. Soon the cottage was filled with the aroma of warm syrup and sizzling batter. Just when she flipped the last pancake, Aidan's hands wrapped around her waist and he nuzzled the back of her ear.

She sighed, turning around with spatula in hand.

"Morning," he whispered.

"Morning."

She searched his face, wondering if he was still angry from the night before. Jade let out her breath, relieved by his sparkling blue eyes in the morning light.

"I'm sorry," he said.

"Sorry about what?"

"I didn't mean to be impatient last night. I just…can't stand the idea of something happening to you, love."

Love? She drew in a breath and he pulled her closer.

"I'm sorry, too. I'm not trying to be stubborn, or what did you say, *g*?"

"You have a good memory, lass." He chuckled, taking her hands in his.

"Thank you for understanding," he said.

He kissed her forehead and smiled.

"Something smells delicious," Aidan said. "What are ye cooking, lass?"

"Pancakes."

"Ach, my favorite!"

"Oh, good! Wasn't sure if you liked them but thought it might be a nice peace offering. Please, have a seat."

She studied his handsome profile, noticing he'd slipped on a white t-shirt and pair of shorts, along with a pair of house slippers.

She brought him a generous plate of flapjacks and offered butter and warmed maple syrup. Afterward, she poured him a cup of coffee and took a seat across from him. Seeing him at her table made her heart skip a beat. She was surprised by how natural it was to start her morning with him.

"So, what do ye have planned for today?" Aidan asked.

"Well, I'm going to the shop after breakfast. I'll be back by six. Anything special you'd like for dinner?"

"Surprise me." He gave her a wink along with his enticing smile. "I have the day off and realized some of yer paint's flaking in the front of the cottage. I'd be happy to help with fixing it. Noticed paint buckets when I put my bag in the hall closet."

"Oh, I don't want to make you work on your day off, Aidan."

"Not a problem. Let's call it an even trade in exchange for your delicious cooking."

"Thank you. I really appreciate it. Been meaning to get to it, but it's been hectic at the shop," Jade said.

"Understandable. You're a busy lady. I was also thinking since I'm home today, you might want to send someone over for the alarm. I can let them in, and it will be set up by the time you get back."

"Oh, that would be brilliant. Thank you!"

"Perfect. Just give me an idea of when they will be stopping by. I might go for a run this morning."

"I sure will," Jade said. She bit down on her lower lip, wondering if she should bring up last night's romantic interlude. Jade imagined things may have turned out quite differently if the sheriff hadn't interrupted. Not knowing how Aidan felt on the matter, she decided to wait.

Aidan helped clean up after breakfast, insisting he'd finish the dishes while she changed for work. She smiled to herself, enjoying the extra help.

WHEN JADE CAME HOME THAT EVENING, SHE WAS WELCOMED BY A FRESH coating of paint on the front exterior of the cottage. She was carrying her groceries down the cobblestone path when Aidan came outside to help. He reached for the bags and gave her a kiss on the cheek.

"Thank you. The cottage looks wonderful," Jade said.

"You're welcome, lass. An alarm company representative stopped by this afternoon," Aidan said as he held the door open with a bright smile. Once they were inside, he gave her instructions on the new setup. She was relieved to have the extra security.

"Are there more groceries in the truck?"

"Just my pumpkins," she said.

"Pumpkins?" His brows rose while he studied her in amusement.

"Yep! It's my favorite time of the year. With everything going on I haven't had a chance to decorate for Halloween."

He followed her to the truck and chuckled when he noticed several large pumpkins in the pickup bed.

"Let me help you with those. Where would you like 'em?"

She smiled, her eyes sparkling. "Let's set them on the porch for now. We can carve some when it's closer to Halloween."

He smiled. Amber light washed over the porch steps while they placed the gourds onto the wooden beams.

"They look lovely against the fresh paint. Thank you, Aidan."

"My pleasure, darlin'." He gave her a peck on the cheek, taking her hand as they walked back inside. Jade put her keys in a crystal bowl by the door and took off her jacket. Aidan met her in the kitchen with a fresh glass of Chardonnay.

"You're spoiling me! I might not let you leave," Jade said.

He grinned watching her move about the kitchen.

"Let me get dinner started. Why don't you relax?" Jade offered.

"Thank you."

He sat down at the dining room table with a glass of wine while she prepared fried tofu and vegetables over saffron rice.

Soon, the rich scents of garlic and zucchini wafted through the cottage. She reached toward the highest shelf, choosing her favorite Scottish china. The set adorned with a delicate thistle design—a precious heirloom from her great-grandmother.

He leaned back in his chair, ocean-blue eyes gleaming in the darkening room while she served him a generous portion of steaming vegetables and rice. Jade took her seat, waiting in anticipation. He spooned up a large bite, relishing the rich flavor.

"It's delicious. I think I could get used to a vegan lifestyle."

"That's what I like to hear."

They spoke amicably about their days, Jade filling him in with stories of interesting customers at the shop and the call to register Morrigan with the State and Aidan about the repairs and observations to her home.

After dinner, Aidan offered to do the dishes like he did the night before. The next evening was equally pleasant and they fell into a comfortable routine.

🙖

JADE ARRIVED HOME ON WEDNESDAY NIGHT TO AN EMPTY COTTAGE. WITH Aidan called to work, she'd taken Dougal and Morrigan to the shop which had the added benefit of drawing in more customers. After punching in her alarm code, she fed the pets and prepared dinner for one. Aidan called to check on Jade before bed. Hearing his voice eased her restless mind. The next couple of days dragged by and she looked forward to seeing him on Saturday morning. While she prepared supper Friday evening, an uneasy feeling washed over her. She'd grown accustomed to Aidan's company and was surprised how his absence affected her.

With the radio blaring, she prepared tacos making sure to leave extra servings in the refrigerator for her favorite new roommate. After the meal, she enjoyed a cup of tea by the fire. Struggling to stay awake, she decided to turn in early. She'd fit an early run on Saturday. The wind was fierce, but absent of rain and thunder that evening. After reading a few chapters of her novel, she snuggled beneath her quilts and surrendered to sleep.

꧁꧂

JUST A FEW MILES FROM THE GIRL'S COTTAGE, BENEATH THE PROTECTION OF the cove, a group of men encircled a raging bonfire.

A gaunt figure hovered close to the burning pyre, chanting in Latin. When the leader finished, he turned to the group, gesturing them closer. A sliver of moonlight slipped from the heavens, illuminating the men on the beach.

"The lass will bring our prey out of hiding. Unfortunately, our plan was nearly foiled by one of you."

The group exchanged worried glances.

"Step forward, lad."

There was a moment of silence. The men waiting in nervous anticipation.

"Reveal yourself." The leader said.

An emaciated figure moved forward, removing his hood to reveal a boyish face. His mouth trembled, his eyes glistening with tears.

"Your actions nearly cost us our freedom, lad. Do you realize what you've done?"

"I…tried to go back. I must have dropped it when we ran away. Please, I beg forgiveness. It won't happen again."

"Silence, fool! The only reason you're still breathing is because of your family's generous funding. Your parents pleaded with me to take you under my wing. Don't make me regret my decision. You're on thin ice."

"Master, I promise it won't happen again. I've done everything you told me to do. I was able to steal the lady's brush from her bedroom. Didn't leave a trace behind! I promise I didn't."

A small smile surfaced on the leader's face. He stepped closer to the boy, stroking gnarled fingers against his hollow cheek. He followed it with a powerful slap across the youth's pale face. The teenager stumbled backward, bellowing in pain. A welt formed before his tears washed over it.

"Get down on your knees."

The boy obeyed, falling to the wet sand, his head bent. His lips twitched in shocked confusion.

"You left the brush behind and the police recovered it."

"I didn't mean to, Master. There wasn't time to go back." He shuddered in the wind.

"You left evidence. The authorities will soon realize someone broke into the lass's cottage. They very well could find our hideout."

The boy swallowed, glancing up towards the hooded figure.

"What will happen to the lady?" The boy asked.

"The lass is of little concern to us. It's the creature we want. An abomination of unholy beings has plagued our race for centuries. Many were killed, but some always seem to find a way to escape. My ancestors gave their lives to eradicate the Unclean Ones. The sacred vow has been passed down from father to son. As Hunters there is no room for mercy in our great quest. You will do well to remember that."

The leader reached into his pocket and retrieved a small tin.

"Lucky for you, I collected strands from the brush before you foolishly misplaced it."

The boy glanced up, a glimmer of hope in his tear-filled eyes. He let out his breath, praying he'd been spared from punishment.

His master retrieved the golden strands, placing them in the palm of his left hand. With his face toward the stars, he chanted in Latin, swaying back and forth to the sound of his own voice. The flames rose in answer. A second cloaked figure stepped forward from the circle and presented him with a ruby encased dagger. The leader received it, whispering an incantation. With one sharp motion, he dragged the edge of the knife over the palm of his hand while tossing the lock of golden hair into the fire. The flames turned blue, blood mixing with the golden tresses.

Afterward, the leader headed to the shore, leaving his followers by the fire. His hands rose to the inky sky, chanting in a foreign tongue. Nearly an hour passed before he returned to the pyre. He walked to the boy, locking eyes with him.

He smiled up at his master, awaiting his fate.

"Strip off your clothes."

The teenager's grin faded.

"Please, sir. Have mercy." His mouth quivered and he glanced toward the other members, hoping someone would intervene. Once again, his prayers had gone unanswered.

"I won't ask again. Disrobe."

With trembling hands, the teenager undressed beneath the starless sky. The black cloak fell to the ground revealing his emaciated form. Shivering, he waited with eyes closed. The leader gestured toward the largest of the group, handing him a long switch of leather. The robed figure stood behind the boy, flicking the switch against his large hand. A whistling sound blew through the icy air.

"Face me, child."

He knelt by his master's feet, with hands outstretched, his tear-filled eyes begging for mercy.

"Begin."

The lash whipped across the boy's scarred back, opening new cuts and tearing old wounds. While his blood flowed freely, high-pitched screams overlapped the rising tides. A smile spread over the master's face watching his apprentice writhing in the sand.

⁂

JADE TOSSED AND TURNED BENEATH THE QUILTS. SHE COULD HEAR DISTANT voices, but the language was undiscernible. Unaware, her bare feet padded along the wooden floorboards while she made her way blindly into the dark. Dougal followed her footsteps, whining while she walked toward the front of the house. The door closed behind her, leaving the terrier barking. His lamenting cries followed her into the night. She listened to hushed voices as she neared the shoreline. Small feet sank beneath dewy sand and the stars paid witness. Icy waves churned against her thighs and hips. When the wind blew through her golden locks, she leaned backward, giving herself to the sea. Her body floated on the currents, drifting toward the horizon. A feeling of peace washed over her; a cloud of orange and black wings hovered in the rosy sky. In wonderment, she watched the kaleidoscope of monarch butterflies disappear into the pink light of dawn. When they were gone, she turned her face toward the shoreline, gasping as she realized that the land had receded unreachably. Recognizing her danger, she flung her arms against the powerful tides, trying desperately to stay afloat. Her legs treaded water, but soon began to tire. Jade swallowed a gulp of salty water while a breaker crashed over her head. Her mouth stretched into a silent scream as she was pulled beneath the dark depths.

Chapter Thirteen

AIDAN DROVE TOWARD JADE'S HOUSE WITH HIS MIND RACING. BEAMS OF light sliced through the thick wall of fog leading toward the cottage. It had been a long shift and he looked forward to a good night's sleep. A friendship deepened into something stronger the past week. It was excruciating being so close, unable to care for her the way he desired.

He found that he enjoyed his new domestic life. He'd lived so long on his own, he didn't realize what he'd been missing. There was a comfort in coming home to rosy cheeks, soft lips, and shapely legs.

He'd kept something important from Jade, and it threatened to destroy their relationship before it ever began, but this morning, he'd made up his mind. He was going to tell her everything and hope for the best. Perhaps she'd understand. If not, at least he'd have tried. Aidan stopped by his penthouse after work. While searching his storage closet, he discovered a box of vintage Halloween decorations. The treasures would surely put a smile on Jade's face. He grinned, imagining her excitement when she opened the box.

After he'd loaded his surprise in the car, Aidan headed back to the cottage. Pink ribbons of light danced across the windshield while he parked on top the cobblestone driveway. As he reached for the container, the sound of Dougal's howls made him jump in his seat. He left the box on the driver's side and raced toward the front door. Once inside, his dog ran in circles trying to get his attention. The fireman called out Jade's name in vain. When she didn't answer, he headed outside with Dougal at his heels. The thick fog made it difficult to see more than a few feet in front of him. The terrier caught the girl's scent and bolted toward the shore. His short legs scattered clumps of sand while he trotted.

"Dougal!" Aidan followed the dog, noticing the fresh footsteps. He tore off his shoes and socks, calling Jade's name. When he reached the shore, an orange and pink sky illuminated golden tresses rising from the currents.

"Jade! My god, she can't swim," he whispered.

Aidan quickly took in the situation, realizing she was going to drown if he didn't get moving. He stripped out of his shirt and trousers and dove into the frigid water. His breaststrokes were strong, but he realized it would be too late by the time he reached her. He watched Jade sink beneath the breaking tides. The thought of losing her was unbearable. Her head was lifted above the water again. He breathed. Then she slipped under and did not rise again.

"Jade!"

A burning sensation gripped his back and legs, seizing his muscles in white-hot agony. Every atom in his body burned. His skin pulsated and throbbed as the metamorphosis began. His spine lengthened, the skin peeling back to reveal a gash of blood and bone. His hips clenched and stretched while his legs melded together. Webbed toes fanned out into four powerful flippers.

When the pain subsided, his lower half was slick and torpedo-shaped. A feeling of peace washed over him. When he dove beneath the icy water, he spotted Jade's body beneath the waves, tossing like a ragdoll in the violent undertow. Once he reached her limp body, his powerful arms pulled her to the surface. Aidan pushed toward the beach fearing he'd been too late. Once they reached the shore, he collapsed next to her lifeless form.

His sealskin contacted with the earth and a fresh bolt of pain ignited in his newly formed flesh. Despite his agony, Aidan rolled Jade to her side and leaned his ear toward her nose, listening for signs of breathing. Realizing she wasn't, he ran his finger inside her mouth searching for debris. Seeing she was clear; he gently pinched her nose shut and sealed his mouth over hers. Her chest rose when he breathed air into her lungs. He checked for a pulse on her slender wrist. Finding none, he repeated the breathing and followed it by chest compressions.

After several minutes, a gush of water poured forth from her gaping mouth. When she vomited into the sand, he moved her onto her side, rubbing her back, pushing her wet hair out of her eyes.

"Jade!"

She blinked in confusion and he let out a sigh of relief.

"Thank god," Aidan said.

Her eyes widened. "What happened to your body?" She pointed a trembling hand toward his back flippers.

As she stared, he groaned, pulling himself onto his elbows, gritting his teeth against the pain. He curled into a fetal position, closing his eyes as his body tore itself apart again. Human legs and feet replaced the blubber. She watched in amazement as the gray flesh melted into swirling vapors beneath the rising sun. When the transformation completed, there was no evidence of what had taken place.

"Aidan," she whispered, unable to catch her breath. He rolled to his side, completely nude. She gazed upon his chiseled body in wonder. While they rested beneath the glow of the orange sky, Aidan's seizures eventually subsided. He reached for his discarded clothes, quickly dressing with his back to her. Once he was clothed, Aidan gathered Jade in his arms.

"I'm so sorry to have kept this secret from you."

"What are you?" she gasped.

"Do you think me a monster?" Aidan asked softly, steeling himself against her reply.

"You saved my life, Aidan. How could I ever consider you a monster?"

Tears of relief stung his eyes. He reached down, kissing her on the forehead. Her fingers played through his damp curls, as powerful arms lifted her from the cold earth. She snuggled against his warm chest, surrendering herself to him.

Aidan carried her back to the cottage as if she weighed nothing. The couple had just returned to the front gate when they heard voices behind them. Two cloaked figures rushed forward. One held a gun while his companion wielded a knife.

"Put the girl down and come with us."

When Aidan turned toward the voice, a third man came from the rear of the cottage. The intruder struck him in the back of the head with a blackjack. He fell to the ground, dropping Jade in the process. She hit her head against a rock, surrendering to a blanket of gray light.

Chapter Fourteen

JADE'S EYES FLUTTERED AS SHE HEARD SIRENS. SHE FELT HERSELF BEING lifted onto a gurney before slipping back into darkness. When she finally regained consciousness, Mary was by her side. Her head pounded when she struggled to sit up in the narrow hospital bed.

"Oh, thank god! You've been out for hours. I was really getting worried," Mary said.

"What happened?" Jade asked.

"There were patrol cars at your house this morning. One of the officers told me you'd been found unconscious with a head injury. They found my number in your wallet."

Jade rubbed at her temple and winced. A large knot had formed on the side of her head. "I'm not sure what happened…"

"It's alright. Why don't you have a drink?" Mary poured water from the plastic pitcher beside her bed and handed her a cup.

Jade drank it down and asked for more.

"God, I'm so thirsty. Feels like I swallowed a bag of table salt."

The women turned as Sheriff Carpenter made his way to the side of the bed.

"Miss Mackenzie, I know you've been through something terrible, but it's important I ask you a few questions regarding your accident. Would you prefer to be alone?"

Glimpses of the near drowning flashed through her mind. She could see Aidan gazing down at her, then the realization that his body was no longer human. The strange seal-like tail was permanently etched in her mind.

"No. No, Mary can stay. Where's Aidan?" Jade said.

"You've been calling out his name in your sleep. Was he with you when you fell?" Sheriff Carpenter asked.

"I fell? I don't recall…everything's so hazy."

"That's perfectly understandable, Miss Mackenzie. My deputies found you unconscious outside your cottage early this morning. We're trying to piece this all together. I tried calling Aidan earlier, but he's not responding. Talked to some of his co-workers about an hour ago. They reported he left the fire station when his shift ended shortly before dawn. Can you recall any details of what transpired?"

Jade rubbed the left side of her head and winced.

"All I remember was floating in the ocean and the next I was sinking. It's all mixed up."

Mary's eyes widened. "What on earth were you doing in the ocean? You can barely swim!"

"I don't know…it's all just a blur."

Sheriff Carpenter nodded. "It's all right. Just take your time. Tell us everything you can remember. Don't leave anything out."

Jade took another sip of water before continuing. "I remember slipping down under the waves…a terrible pain in my chest. The next thing I knew, I was looking up at Aidan. He was so worried."

"He…" she hesitated, afraid to mention his body was no longer human. They'd think she'd lost her mind if she suggested her friend was a selkie. "I can only remember bits and pieces. All I know for certain is Aidan saved my life. I would have drowned if he hadn't rescued me. He carried me back to the cottage. We were about to walk through the front gate when we heard the voices." She closed her eyes trying to focus. "Oh, god! Men! There were men there, who attacked us! They had weapons…a gun and a knife." Jade covered her face with her hands, shuddering at the memory.

Sheriff Carpenter leaned close. "Take a breath, Miss Mackenzie. We'll take this nice and slow. Do you remember how many there were?"

"It's…all so fuzzy. She rubbed at her temples, trying to recall the imagery to mind. "One of them had a deep voice. He was the one with the gun."

Mary gasped, her eyes widening like a frightened cat.

"That's very good, Jade," Sheriff Carpenter said.

"The second man had a knife. He was shorter, but not by much. They were both...tall. Really tall. They were wearing black hooded cloaks. I couldn't see more. They seemed to come out of nowhere."

Sheriff Carpenter's pursed his lips. "Our deputy found you outside the cottage. You were unconscious. Dougal was by your side."

"Something must have happened to Aidan," Jade said. Her eyes filled with tears of frustration and she shook her head. "He saved me, and I couldn't help him."

Mary moved closer to the bed. "What on earth were you doing out in the ocean to begin with? I remember that time we went camping at Lake Shasta. You wouldn't even get your feet wet."

"I know, it was like a terrible dream. I would have drowned if Aidan hadn't swum after me. He must have given me CPR. I remember coughing up water. I was so weak and dizzy." She looked at their concerned faces, wanting to explain more but afraid they wouldn't believe her, or worse, think she lost her mind.

Sheriff Carpenter smiled gently. "You're doing fine, Jade. Everything you've told me is very helpful. They sound like the same men spotted on your property a few days ago."

Her lips trembled when she recalled Aidan's warning. He said something terrible might happened if she stayed at the cottage and now it had. The worst part was that he was paying the price for her stubbornness.

Mary sat down next to her on the bed. "We'll find him, sweetie."

Tears rolled down her cheeks and she struggled to get out of bed.

"Jade, you need to rest. The doctors want to run more tests. You might have a concussion," Mary said.

As her friend took her hand, she reluctantly moved her legs back under the blanket.

"If your tests check out, they should be releasing you sometime this afternoon." Mary said.

"Oh, no. What about Dougal and Morrigan? Has anyone been feeding them?" Jade suddenly cried.

"Don't worry," Mary said soothingly. "They're fine. I already fed them and let Dougal out to potty. I arrived at the cottage early this morning. Your door was unlocked, and the alarm was disabled. I figured I better feed the animals before I left for the hospital. Sheriff Carpenter said it would be alright once they searched the cottage. I found your keys in a crystal bowl. I locked the door afterward but wasn't sure how to set the alarm."

"Thank you so much. It's a relief knowing the animals are alright."

Sheriff Carpenter closed his notebook and stood up.

"Miss Mackenzie, we still have patrol units monitoring your house. With Aidan away and in light of the assault and kidnapping, I've changed it to a twenty-four-hour watch."

She nodded, now grateful for the extra security.

"I appreciate it, Sheriff. Aidan tried to warn me how dangerous it was staying at the cottage. I should have listened. He's gone and it's all my fault."

Tears spilled over her pale cheeks; her body trembled beneath the hospital sheets. The shock of the attack finally caught up with her.

"It's not your fault, Jade. We're going to find Aidan. Just make sure you keep locked up and use the security system when you get home," Sheriff Carpenter said.

He reached into his shirt pocket and handed her his business card.

"Please call me if you remember anything else. I'll be in touch."

"Thank you, Sheriff."

After he left, Mary sat next to Jade in the chair by the bed. Jade gingerly touched the knot on the side of her head.

"Thank god they found you. What on earth were you doing out in the ocean?"

"I'm really not sure. I went to bed last night early, and the next thing I remember is floating in the sea. It was horrible. I feel like I'm seriously losing my mind."

"Do you suppose you might have sleepwalked?" Mary asked.

"Maybe…it's all so strange. She lowered her voice to a whisper. "There's more to the story, Mary. I just couldn't tell the sheriff. He just needs to focus on finding Aidan."

"I had the feeling you were holding something back. What else happened?"

She glanced around the room, making sure they were alone. "I'll explain everything once we get back to the cottage. I'm grateful you're here with me. I don't think I could bear the sight of my empty house right now."

"Of course. I'll stay as long as you need me."

Jade received a battery of tests including a CAT scan before being released from the hospital. She'd suffered a slight concussion but was expected to enjoy a full recovery. Dr. Edward Green, the hospital's chief attending, made sure to stop by to check on Jade before releasing her into Mary's care. The women listened politely while the elderly physician explained the effects of a concussion and what things to avoid. After he gave Jade a prescription and answered her questions, Mary helped her friend change into her street clothes and pushed her in a wheelchair to the pharmacy. After picking up a prescription of pain medication, the ladies left the hospital. Jade waited while Mary went to fetch the car.

The fog was unusually thick that afternoon, so Mary drove under the speed limit. When the women turned onto the trail leading to the cottage, they spotted a police cruiser parked nearby.

"Well, at least you have security," Mary said.

"Yes, I suppose." The guilt of Aidan's kidnapping weighed heavily on Jade's mind. She'd never forgive herself if tragedy befell him. Jade said a silent prayer as they parked outside.

After they entered the cottage, Jade locked the door and showed Mary how to set up the security system.

"The code is 'Morrigan' spelled out on the numbers."

Mary nodded her head. Dougal, hearing them, rushed over wagging his tail. Morrigan cawed from the bedroom.

"Let's get you outside for a potty break, buddy," Jade said.

The women watched the churning sea while Dougal went about his business. A few moments later, the dog came back with something in his mouth.

"What do you have, boy?" Jade asked.

He dropped a cotton handkerchief by her feet.

As she reached for the linen, her eyes stung with tears. She studied Aidan's crest embroidered on the corner of the cloth.

"What is it?" Mary asked.

"It belongs to Aidan. One of his handkerchiefs. He told me the other day his mother gifted him a monogram set before she left to visit his aunt in Scotland. It was her last gift."

"That's heartbreaking," Mary said.

Jade nodded, holding the handkerchief to her face. The pleasant aroma of aftershave still lingered.

Mary placed her hand on her friend's back.

"We'll find him."

Jade nodded. They headed back to the cottage, locking the door behind. On the way to her bedroom, Jade glanced up at the fireplace mantel. "Oh my god!"

"I know. I wasn't sure how to tell you."

The man in the portrait was now submerged, only the top of his head still visible above the waves. Jade stepped closer to the painting, realizing the sealskin was no longer on the beach.

Jade's lips trembled while she studied the portrait. "I need to tell you something, Mary."

"I want to hear everything, but before you get started, why don't you take a hot shower and change into some comfy pajamas. You've been through a terrible ordeal and need to rest. Doctor's orders."

"That actually sounds like a lovely idea," Jade said.

"Good. I'll make a pot of tea, and we can figure this all out."

"Thank you."

Jade went to her bedroom to collect her pajamas. Once inside the bathroom, she stripped off her sweatpants and t-shirt and stood shivering on the cold tiles. She turned on the faucet above her clawfoot tub and poured in a generous amount of rose scented bubble bath. Once the tub was ready, she slipped into the steamy foam. As she closed her eyes, images of the near drowning flashed through her mind as the fuzziness in her mind cleared and the memories returned. She shuddered, biting down on her bottom lip, recalling Aidan's beautiful blue eyes burning with pain. What she'd witnessed was unimaginable. Watching his body transform from seal to human was strangely beautiful. He was majestic in his metamorphosis. Her mind drifted while she concentrated on her breath, leaning back against the headrest. After she'd dried off and changed, she headed over to the fireplace with a towel wrapped around her damp curls. The logs in the fireplace crackled, a gusty wind rattled the insides of the chimney.

A few moments later, the shriek of the tea kettle sounded from the kitchen. Mary carried a silver tray filled with a fresh pot of tea, a pitcher of almond milk, and bowl of sugar over to the table by the fireplace.

Jade blew away the steam from her mug, resting her head on the back of the couch while Dougal laid his head on top of her fuzzy slippers.

"I thought it was all a dream. The tides were...calling my name. The next thing I knew, I was floating. A cloud of butterflies hovered above my head. There were hundreds, maybe thousands of monarchs. They filled the dusky sky with their beautiful orange and black wings. They were so close; I could see the powder on their wings. I closed my eyes...it was just so peaceful. When I opened my eyes, the butterflies were gone. It was peaceful until I noticed my distance from the shore. I think that's when I realized it was real, because I felt afraid. When I'd dreamed this before, there wasn't any fear. Suddenly, there was only darkness. The waves crashed over my head and I went under. I struggled, finally managing to make it back to the surface. The shore was so far away, but I could see Aidan. He was calling my name. There's no way he could have reached me in time. I tried to tread water, but something kept pulling me downward. Eventually, I couldn't fight any more. I sank beneath the waves, holding my breath until I couldn't anymore. It was so cold, Mary. When I opened my mouth, it felt like a thousand knives pierced my chest. I stared into the depths of the sea and saw his face. Aidan's beautiful blue eyes were wide with fear. And... he'd changed."

"What do you mean?

"His upper body appeared normal, but his bottom half was like a seal."

"Jade, you almost drowned. Maybe your mind was just playing tricks on you. We've been talking so much about selkie legends lately. You probably hallucinated from oxygen deprivation."

"I know what I saw, Mary. It was clear as day, and I had a second look when I regained consciousness. He must have given me CPR after we reached shore because I remember coughing up so much water. Once I caught my breath, Aidan helped me sit up. That's when I realized his body was no longer human. I asked him what was happening, but he started to have a seizure. It was terrible. One moment he was talking and the next he was writhing in the sand. I watched his sealskin stretch and bubble off to reveal until it...sloughed human legs and feet. Then it dissolved in the sunlight, Mary. After he rested, Aidan dressed and carried me home because I was still so weak. We had just reached the cottage gate when the men appeared."

"Oh my god, Jade. How terribly frightening for you! Do you suppose these men belong to the cult Aidan mentioned earlier? The one persecuting his family?" Mary asked.

"I have a hunch they're part of the same group. What if they try to hurt or kill him?" She touched the gash on the side of her head and winced.

"Let me get you some ice," Mary said. She returned with a bag of frozen peas and a hand towel. "Try to hold this against the swelling."

"Thank you." She placed the bag on the side of her head and closed her eyes.

Mary returned with Jade's prescription and a glass of water. "Go ahead and take these. You really need to rest."

Dougal licked her hand and she leaned back on the couch.

"The sheriff has a team of officers searching for Aidan. I'm sure they know what they're doing," Mary said.

"I just feel like it's all my fault. If I hadn't insisted on staying at the cottage, none of this would have happened. Aidan practically begged me to go back to his penthouse. I refused and now he's been taken." Tears rolled down her cheeks and she wrapped her arms around her knees.

Mary sat next to Jade, rubbing her friend's shoulder. Morrigan flew from her perch, landing on the couch. She nuzzled her beak against her mistress' pajama top.

"It's important for you to rest. There's nothing you can do right now. When you're feeling better, we'll start our investigation in the evenings after work. I'd be happy to help at the store tomorrow. I know it sounds harsh, but you know the first year of a new business is the hardest and it won't do you any good if this fails," Mary said.

Jade was not sure how she could go back to work after everything that transpired, but she was touched by Mary's support.

"I really appreciate everything. I know you're losing time at your gallery."

"I have coverage this weekend. Some of my employees finished their midterms early. Besides, you're my family and this is an emergency." She poured her friend another cup of tea. Jade's eyes were heavy as she drained the cup. Mary covered her with a quilt while she dozed by the fireplace.

Chapter Fifteen

AIDAN BLINKED HIS EYES OPEN, WINCING AS THE POUNDING IN THE BACK OF his head became stronger. A trickle of light streamed from a small tear on the newspaper-covered window. Within the ray of sunshine sat a gray rat. The rodent washed its whiskers with tiny pink hands before scurrying into the shadows. A heavy scent of mold lingered in the musty air. While he tried focusing on the unfamiliar surroundings, his thoughts turned to Jade.

Where is she?

He attempted to stand and was immediately restricted by shackles around his legs and arms. Everything came back in a flood of memories. Jade in the ocean, his body changing, the pain, the shedding of skin, the metamorphosis. *It hadn't happened in years.*

"Jade!"

The door to the room opened. A hooded figure came forward flanked by two bodyguards. The leader removed his cloak revealing ashen skin mapped by ropes of twisted scars. His milky right eye was a startling contrast to the empty left socket. The corner of his mouth twitched while he studied Aidan.

"Creature, your days are numbered. You should make peace with whatever your kind considers God."

"Who are you? Where's Jade?" Aidan shouted.

"The girl is of no concern to us. We've been searching for the Unclean Ones for centuries. *Your* family," the man sneered, "we were told perished at sea when they tried to flee justice. It was a fitting end. But our numbers had seen visitors come to the MacFie castle for years and were finally able to track down your line. Your very existence is blasphemy to the eyes of Our Creator. When we're done with you, we will return to Scotland to finish the final reaping before the birth of more Unclean Ones taint the face of God's holy earth."

"You're talking nonsense! I don't know what you're talking about! Where's Jade? What have you done with her?"

The leader ignored his questions and continued with his monologue. "When the Hunter's Moon rises, your life will be taken, and your powers released."

Aidan stared blankly. "What powers do you think I have? I'm a fireman!"

"Don't play games with me, creature. Do you pretend ignorance? Our families have been at war for centuries. My ancestors followed yours to the New World. They were successful in weeding out your family members including your mother and father."

Aidan's face flared at the mention of his parents. The leader regarded his prisoner closely. "Do you really think your parents died in an airplane crash? Don't you think it's odd their bodies were never recovered? That you never had any cousins or family? We ensured that there were as few of you abominations as possible, whittling you down until our task could be completed."

Aidan clenched his fists and tried to stand. "You bastard! How dare you suggest such a thing. It was an accident!"

The chains around his legs pulled painfully against his exposed skin. The thought that his parents might have been murdered made his blood boil. He yearned to grab his captor by his throat and make him take back his words. *It simply couldn't be.*

The elderly man grinned while his prisoner fought against the restraints. The image was gruesome considering only the right side of his mouth moved when he smiled, the left having been melded together in a tangle of knotted scars. Now the fireman's mind raced, his survival training kicked into gear. He'd been in numerous close calls in his time in the field and he realized he wouldn't have a chance to escape if he lost control. His eyes scanned the dimly lit room, taking in the details. The bodyguards were massive. He sized them up, trying to find the weakest link. They appeared to be brothers—both possessed the same dull expressions, their blank stares suggesting that they both were simple-mindedly loyal and devoted.

Then Aidan's eyes fell on a gangly teenager lingering in the back. He appeared nervous and unsure. Perhaps, if he could find out why he was there, the boy might help him escape.

The leader gestured to the young man with the back of his hand. "Feed the creature, Finnean."

The boy came forward holding a tray filled with half-cooked potatoes, stale bread, and water. He placed it next to Aidan's legs avoiding eye contact. Afterward, the minions followed their leader into the hallway and bolted the door. Aidan's mind raced, trying to make sense of things. The mere mention of his parents infuriated him. A silent rage coursed through his veins when he pictured his captor's disformed face. How he'd love to get his hands on him. He shook his head, trying to control his temper. Aidan closed his eyes, replaying the strange conversation in his mind. Was he the last of his kind or where there more like him? If so, where were they?

The leader mentioned going back to Scotland for the Final Reaping. That would happen soon. *This implied other selkies were alive and well.*

He realized his questions were of little relevance if he couldn't find a way to escape. He tried to push away his mounting fear and concentrate on the situation at hand.

It was difficult focusing when his mind drifted back to Jade. Was she a prisoner locked away in another room? If so, he needed to help her. These men were dangerous, possibly capable of murder. An overwhelming feeling of rage emboldened him when he considered their possible involvement in his parents' death. If only he'd known the stories of Hunters to be as true as his family's supernatural form, he would have found a way to protect them. He wouldn't allow it to happen again. He'd willingly give his life to protect Jade's. She had nothing to do with this. The thought of her in danger because of him made his stomach clench. *Please let her be safe.*

Aidan glanced down at the chains around his ankles. He tested the restraints, pulling and pushing against the rusted metal. A narrow band of light revealed slight cracks in the plaster around the manacles. If he worked long enough, there might be a chance to break free. He spent the remainder of the afternoon and evening fighting the chains until his skin dripped with blood.

Chapter Sixteen

Jade followed her friend's advice and went back to the shop a couple of days after her accident. Mary insisted Jade take it easy in the backroom while she helped customers up front. While she sorted through new merchandise, Jade's mind wandered. She called the police station in the morning and again at noon. Sheriff Carpenter tried to ease her worries, insisting all available officers were working the case. She glanced at her phone for what must have been the fiftieth time that day. No new messages.

Her nerves were on edge while she worked. Shortly before closing, Jade gathered the receipts and totaled the day's earnings. While she focused on the numbers, a cool hand touched her shoulder. She turned in surprise, gazing into ebony eyes flickering in the dimming light.

"Young lady, it's lovely to see you again."

Jade forced a smile, trying to hide her uneasiness.

"It's very nice to see you, Madame Garnier. Can I help you with something?"

"Well, dear, I think you may be the one who needs my help."

"Oh?"

"Why, yes. I was wondering if you still had my card. I'd expected to have heard from you by now."

Jade shifted her feet, uncomfortable by the elderly woman's penetrating gaze.

"I'm not quite sure what you're talking about?"

"Miss Mackenzie, I sense you're searching for answers. I had a strong feeling the day we met. You see, I'm psychic. I may be able to help you with whatever is troubling you. I can't help but notice the pain in your pretty gray eyes."

"That's very kind, but I really don't know if anyone can help me at this point."

Madame Garnier took Jade's hand in hers. "You've provided me such joy with my lovely teapot. Let me return the favor with a little reading. What's the harm?"

"A reading?"

"Why, yes. I believe a Tarot card session would be useful for you. Perhaps we can come to an understanding."

The bell jingled when Mary entered the shop with Dougal by her side, sending an orange flash of light to jump through the store. Morrigan cawed from her perch as her ivory feathers shone amber. Mary untied Dougal's leash and the terrier rushed toward the counter.

"Oh, hello," Mary said.

Jade smiled, locking eyes meaningfully with her friend. "You remember Madame Garnier from the grand opening?"

"Why yes, of course," Mary said.

"It's nice to see you again, young lady. We were just discussing a Tarot card appointment at my home. You're welcome to join us if you'd like. The more the merrier," Madame Garnier said. The young women exchanged glances.

"You're going to have a psychic reading, Jade?" Mary said, with her brow raised.

"I don't know. Madame Garnier just offered."

The senior citizen folded her hands together and smiled. "How about this? You both may drop by any time after 6pm. I'll give you the friends and family discount."

Jade shrugged noncommittally. She would have laughed at the idea a few days ago. Now, all her beliefs and convictions had gone out the window. She'd seen her friend turn into a selkie, her painting change before her eyes, and strange men in black hoods were stealing beloved heirlooms from her cottage. A Tarot reading? It seemed tame compared to the past weeks.

"It couldn't hurt," Mary said. "At least it's something to take your mind off things."

"That's true," Jade said.

"So, it's a yes?" Madame Garnier asked.

Jade nodded. "Sure, let's do it."

"Wonderful. I think you will be quite pleased."

The psychic reached into her purse and scribbled the address on the back of her business card.

"I'm just down the street. See you after six." She wrapped her black-laced shawl around her frail shoulders and made her way out. Dougal followed her to the door, wagging his tail as she disappeared into the autumn light.

After the women closed the shop for the day, they headed to Mary's car.

"I can wait with Dougal and Morrigan while you go inside for your reading. That way, you won't have to go back to the cottage to drop them off," Mary said.

"Sounds good. Are you sure you don't want a Tarot reading?"

Mary shook her head and giggled. "I'm good, but thanks for the offer. Either it will help or be entertaining, but I'm not interested."

Jade placed the bird's carrier in the back seat while Dougal hung his head out the window, his tongue rolling out the side of his mouth.

Mary entered the address in the car's navigation system and followed the directions to Madame Garnier's home. They parked outside a small bungalow a few blocks from the antique shop. The front yard was littered with potted plants and plastic flamingos. A neon sign that said "Psychic" flickered in the bay window.

Jade shook her head, wondering what she'd got herself into.

She tapped on the door and waited. Several moments later, the elderly woman escorted her inside a candlelit parlor. Madame Garnier now wore a black Victorian gown frilled with lace. Jade's eyes widened while she looked about the room. Black cats covered every surface including the chairs and table. Their eyes flickered with curiosity as she walked past them. The house was aglow with pewter candelabras and Himalayan salt lamps. A strong aroma of incense hung in the air. *This woman is either very dedicated, or completely crazy!* thought Jade.

The psychic gestured toward a seat at the dining room table. Once Jade sat down, her eyes darted about the dark room. An ebony cat purred against her legs when Madame Garnier took her seat. The psychic placed three stacks of cards in front of her and closed her eyes. Candlelight reflected her shrouded face. She pushed back her veil, dark eyes glimmering in the hazy light.

"Women are intuitive. Some more than others," Madame Garnier said. The elderly woman considered the young woman across the table. "You seem anxious, dear. Are you needing to get back soon?"

"I'm afraid I don't have a lot of time tonight," Jade said hesitantly.

"How about this, young lady: We will do one card today. It will be short and sweet."

"Yes, that would be fine." Relief washed over her, wanting desperately to leave. She watched Madame Garnier's arthritic hands moving over her deck of cards.

"Miss Mackenzie, I'd like you to close your eyes."

Jade reluctantly did as asked wishing to be anywhere but this strange house.

"Think about what you desire. Perhaps there's a question you'd like answers to? Meditate a moment. When you open your eyes, I will have you choose your Tarot card for today's reading. Any questions?"

Jade shook her head, keeping her eyes closed.

"Very good," Madame Garnier said.

Jade sat back in her chair, imagining Aidan's blue eyes. She wanted desperately to find him. While she listened to the cats purring around the room, their soothing sounds lulled her into a meditative state. Soft bodies brushed against her legs as they wove themselves under her chair. The flames of the candles flickered, and a warm breeze blew past her face.

"Are you ready?" Madame Garnier asked.

Jade nodded.

The psychic gathered the three decks together and placed them into one stack. She tapped the top card before shuffling, then fanned the Tarot cards in a wide arch.

"You may open your eyes now, Miss Mackenzie."

Jade studied the back of the cards with interest. The design seemed familiar—an orange butterfly centered on top the ebony background. The images were upright, facing away from the dealer.

"Please choose one card, Miss Mackenzie."

Her fingers grazed over the deck, then stopped when they reached the end. She pulled her card.

"Please turn it over."

Jade did as she was told.

The psychic's eyes widened while studying the symbol. "Very interesting. The card you pulled is the Reversed Moon. You've been going through quite an ordeal of late, but things are beginning to change. A door is opening; don't be afraid to pass through. It feels like you've doubted your intuition for far too long. I felt it the day I met you at your grand opening. You're sensitive. Have you been having strange dreams lately?"

"Yes," Jade said apprehensively.

"This does not surprise me. You must listen to this inner voice. Behold the Tarot card. Notice the towers and the light mirroring the sun. There is a small pool in the foreground, see? It represents the unconscious. A small crayfish is emerging, crawling from the depths. This represents the beginning of the unconsciousness unfolding. There's a wolf nearby. This animal represents the tame and untamed aspects of the mind. Perhaps you find yourself questioning your reality, Miss Mackenzie?"

Jade leaned forward and nodded. "There's been very strange things happening to me over the past few months. They've made me question everything I once held to be true. Nothing seems to make sense anymore."

The psychic nodded, placing her gnarled fingers over Jade's. "Listen to your intuition. It must never be ignored. This is your guide. Your dreams are a doorway to the unconscious both past and present. I have some homework for you today."

Jade glanced up with her brow knit. "Oh?"

"I'd like you to purchase a journal. Place it by your bed tonight. Write down the dreams the moment you wake. Make sure to include all details, even ones which seem insignificant. You may find that you learn from what your unconscious has to tell you."

Jade smiled. "Umm, thank you. I think I'll take your advice about the journal. It couldn't hurt."

"Very well, dear."

Madame Garnier was quiet while she placed the Tarot card back in the deck. She closed her eyes for a moment in meditation.

"Your reading is now over. Short and sweet."

"Already?" Jade smiled. "That was actually kind of fun and a lot faster that I thought it would be. How much do I owe you?"

"Let's make the first one free," Madame Garnier said benevolently.

"Are you sure?"

"Yes, I'm sure. Please let me know how things turn."

"I definitely will," Jade said.

The elderly woman escorted her to the front steps as three black cats weaved between her ankles.

Jade walked toward her friend's car and Mary rolled down the window.

"How did it go?"

"It was interesting. Madame Garnier suggested I buy a journal to jot down my dreams. She thinks they can reveal something. Do you mind if we stop at Target on the way home? I might pick one up tonight."

"Sure. I guess it can't hurt, you know. Journaling your anxiety and all that," Mary offered supportively.

The women finished some shopping before going back to the cottage. After dinner, they continued their research, looking for clues to Aidan's disappearance. It was close to midnight before Mary closed her laptop.

"We could go all night like this. Maybe we should get some sleep," Mary said.

Jade nodded and rose to go to bed. "Goodnight, Mary. Thank you."

Morrigan and Dougal were fast asleep by the time she was under the covers. She tossed and turned for over an hour before falling into a fitful sleep.

JADE WALKED DOWN A TRAIL COVERED IN AUTUMN LEAVES. SHE GLANCED UP, *noticing a sliver of moonlight slipping through a cluster of eucalyptus trees. Monarch butterflies covered the branches nestled together in tight clusters. Long shadows followed her footsteps. When she was about to turn back from the trail, she heard a man's familiar voice.*

"Aidan?" she called.

She followed the sound which led to a row of abandoned houses. The decrepit buildings were separated from the trail by a rusty chain link fence. A high-pitched cawing made her jump backward. She gasped when she spotted her raven perching on top of an abandoned house.

"Morrigan?"

The bird answered by flapping her ivory wings in the fading light. Jade approached the metal barrier and frowned. Realizing she'd need to walk around the entire block to get to the frontside, she decided to try to climb the fence instead. She noticed a hole in the middle, so she wedged the tip of her sneaker inside and pulled herself up. Once she straddled the top, she hooked her left foot on the opposite side. She dropped toward the ground, landing awkwardly into a pile of leaves and branches. She rushed toward the house as Morrigan hopped through the open door.

The home was damp and musky, with newspapers covering the windows. She dodged past piles of trash strewn over warped floorboards. She followed the sound of flapping wings toward the back of the house and then through an open door. Once outside, her eyes widened in disbelief. Garnet rays showered the rising tides drifting toward the sandy hillside.

This is impossible, *she told herself.* The beach is several blocks away. It can't be this close.

Jade gasped, noticing a group of men encircling a pyre. Ribbons of smoke twirled toward the starless sky. The leader turned his attention toward the shore while a man was dragged kicking and screaming across the dunes. Her breath hitched, realizing the captive was Aidan. His captors paused by the water's edge long enough to place a rope around his neck. She raced toward the crashing waves calling his name.

He struggled against his restraints, turning toward the sound of her voice. His piercing eyes caught the shine of fading sun. The leader of the group stood over his body, dagger in hand. There was a flash of metal before the jagged blade sliced through flesh and bone. His screams of agony drowned out her own.

Chapter Seventeen

JADE SAT UP IN BED WHILE BEADS OF SWEAT ROLLED DOWN HER PALE FACE. Her hand trembled against the lamp switch. She took a deep breath, brushing the damp curls from her forehead. After the thrumming of her heart slowed to a normal pace, she reached for her new journal and began jotting down the details of her nightmare. There was something important about the butterflies. She realized there was a connection between the monarchs and Aidan's whereabouts. This was the second time she'd had a dream with both of them. It didn't make sense, but she knew deep down they were related. What had the psychic told her? *Listen to your hunches.*

She was too unsettled by her dream to go back to bed, so she took a shower and changed into a pair of jeans, t-shirt, and hoodie. She wrote a quick note to Mary, leaving it on the kitchen table beneath a crystal flower vase.

Dougal trotted over, then began whimpering when she made her way toward the front door.

"You stay here, sweetie. I'll be back soon. Mary will take good care of you."

She grabbed her keys and headed outside. Dawn was just making its debut in a dazzling display of pink and purple hues. Jade drove toward Starbuck's to pick up a mocha from their drive-through. She wasn't exactly sure where she was headed, but she knew she had to find some butterflies.

DOUGAL'S WHIMPERING SOON TURNED TO ANGUISHED HOWLS. MARY AWOKE to the sound but was too tired to get out of bed. She pulled the pillow over her head, snuggling deeper under the covers and away from the sudden draft. The next thing she knew it was mid-morning. She yawned and stretched, slipping on her robe and a pair of fuzzy slippers. She noticed the note on the kitchen table when she headed to the kitchen to make coffee.

> *Good morning, Mary,*
>
> *I just wanted to let you know I've gone out for a drive. I left early and hope I didn't wake you. I had a pretty restless night with some vivid dreams. I think I'll drive around for a bit; hopefully, something will click.*
>
> *My hunches are always freshest in the morning. I had the craziest dream about monarch butterflies last night. I won't go into details, but they led me to Aidan.*
>
> *Crazy, right? I'll explain more when I get home. I'll try to be back before lunch. Would you mind giving Dougal a potty break and his breakfast? There's some fresh mash in the fridge for Morrigan. Thank you! I should be home in a couple hours.*
>
> *Talk soon*
> *~Jade*

Mary shook her head after reading the note. She prepared a pot of coffee and set out Dougal's bowl. He refused to eat, choosing to pace in front of the door. The terrier scratched anxiously at the barrier.

"I'll be back in a minute, Morrigan."

The raven cawed from the bedroom in answer.

Half awake, Mary opened the front door to let Dougal outside. While she turned toward the porch, a blur of ivory wings shot past her face. She watched in horror when Morrigan flew over the sand dunes, disappearing into the thick fog.

"Oh, no! Morrigan!"

She hurried back inside, slipped on her shoes, and snapped a leash on Dougal. They rushed down to the sand, Mary calling frantically for the lost raven. She spent the next couple of hours running up and down the beach calling the bird's name.

"This isn't happening," she whispered over and over.

How could I have been so careless. Jade will be devastated when she comes back. Mary decided to drive up the road, hoping to see if the raven was nearby.

She drove for hours, searching for both Morrigan and Jade. She called Jade's phone repeatedly. Each time it went to voicemail. After what seemed like an eternity, she headed back to the cottage hoping that her friend had returned. Her heart sunk when she realized neither Jade's truck nor Morrigan were back, despite the fact that it was well past the time Jade should have returned for lunch. While the car idled, she rested her forehead against the steering wheel. Mary felt the sharp edges of panic close in around her. Dougal, sensing her distress, snuggled close, resting his face on her lap. She gave him a pat as he thumped his tail against the car seat.

"Let's try the police station, boy. It's the only thing I can think of right now."

Her mind raced as they drove. She led the dog inside and asked for Sheriff Carpenter at the front desk.

Mary paced back and forth in the waiting room, letting out a sigh of relief when Sheriff Carpenter arrived.

"Hello, Miss Deane. Let's go on back to my office so we can talk."

"Thank you, Sheriff. Would it be alright to bring Dougal?"

"Of course."

Sheriff Carpenter reached down and gave the dog a scratch behind his ears. He thumped his tail on the polished floor.

"Thanks. I didn't want to leave him in the car," Mary said.

The terrier trotted alongside the pair as they headed to Sheriff Carpenter's office. The seasoned officer shut the door behind them and gestured to a leather seat facing his desk. Jade pushed her manicured nails through her bobbed hair, trying to organize her thoughts. She quickly relayed everything that had happened that morning, then handed Jade's note to the sheriff.

He looked over the paper and nodded. "It's too early to officially name this a missing person's case."

"I was afraid of that," Mary said.

"There's a few possibilities. Jade might just be taking her time looking for Aidan. She may have left her phone charger behind. And some of the town's reception is spotty. With that said, it does concern me you've been unable to reach her." He folded his hands together. "I have an idea."

Sheriff Carpenter paged one of his officers. Several minutes later a deputy in his late twenties came through the door. He was well over six feet tall with a dirty-blond crewcut and piercing green eyes. Mary imagined he didn't miss many gym appointments.

He flashed a warm smile when they were introduced.

"Deputy Rheinstein, you've been briefed on the MacFie case?"

"Yes, it's a real shame. I've known Aidan for a long time. He's a good friend."

"That's why I think you'd be the perfect officer for this situation."

The deputy's eyebrows rose in question.

"Mary has reason to believe Jade Mackenzie might be in danger. She left early this morning and has not been in contact, which is unusual for her. She left a note behind." Sheriff Carpenter handed the paper to his officer. The deputy's forehead wrinkled while he studied it.

"It does sound a little odd, nothing concrete, but we've gone on hunches before. Remember when Madame Garnier worked on the Gallagher case last year?"

"I do," Sheriff Carpenter said. "She's been a real asset over the years."

Mary glanced between the two men. "The psychic works for your department?"

"More like a consultant. Do you know her?" Sherriff Carpenter asked.

"We met at the antique shop. Jade went to see her last night for a reading. It's not something she'd normally do, but Madame Garnier suggested she might be able to help her. That's why Jade journaled her dreams last night. The psychic believed it might lead her to Aidan."

"Interesting," Sheriff Carpenter said. He turned toward his deputy. "I'd like you to escort Miss Deane around town today. See if you can come up with anything."

The deputy studied Mary's face, lingering just a little longer than necessary. "It'd be my pleasure, ma'am."

"Thank you. I really appreciate your help."

The officer escorted Mary outside to his patrol car. They glanced up at the darkening sky and readied themselves for another storm.

Chapter Eighteen

JADE DROVE FOR SEVERAL HOURS LOST IN THOUGHT. AFTER DAYS OF NO leads, she needed to get out of the cottage, do something to find Aidan. Leaving the house at dawn wasn't the most rational choice. She figured Mary would be shaking her head reading her note. Her friend liked to think things through, map out a plan, and stick to it. Jade was more of a fly-by-the-seat-of-her-pants kind of girl. Just like the shop in Pacific Grove. She hadn't even organized a solid business strategy before moving to Pacific Grove. All she knew was she had a desire to run a shop, a little money from her inheritance, a mortgage-free place to lay her head, and a strong knowledge of antiques.

Her mother and grandmother had introduced her at a young age an appreciation for everything vintage. She could tell the difference from a rare collectible, or a worthless piece of kitsch at a glance. So, she'd thrown caution to the wind and made the plunge. What was the worst that could happen? She'd lose all her savings and the shop? Sure. But the possible positive outcomes were well worth the gamble in her eyes. After all, you only live once, she told herself. And life could be cut short at any moment. She knew this from the personal tragedy of losing both her mother and father before the age of twenty-five.

She hadn't considered paranormal activity a contributing factor in her life. Being stalked by cult members and falling for a handsome selkie was also something she hadn't accounted for. Were her feelings genuine? Could she be falling in love with a nonhuman being? A hybrid of some sort? These thoughts made her dizzy. Could it be she was just overreacting to the circumstances in which she now found herself? A near-death experience can really mess with one's emotions, after all.

Had her mind played tricks on her? Aidan couldn't be an actual selkie, right? Her thoughts wandered back to his divinely beautiful aquamarine eyes, his beguiling smile. The way she felt when he touched her. No one even came close to making her feel the things he did. His kiss set her soul on fire.

Yes, she knew without a shadow of a doubt that she loved the man. And realizing what real love looked like changed her perspective on everything.

Did Aidan feel the same way? She hoped so. All Jade knew was she had to find him before something terrible happened. She shuddered recalling the dream. The knife coming down upon his skin, sawing through flesh and bone.

Focus.

She drove for hours, aimlessly. It was nearing dusk by the time she was getting ready to give up and head back home. When she drove down Lighthouse Avenue, she noticed a flash of orange and black darting past the windshield. The kaleidoscope of monarchs flew toward a grove of trees across the road. Her heart pounded while she pursued their flight.

Jade spotted a green sign for Monarch Grove Sanctuary. She followed the arrow, driving down a gravely road leading to an empty parking lot. After locking her truck, she strolled across an acorn strewn path cutting through the sanctuary. Pine, cypress, and eucalyptus trees lined the empty walkway. Vibrant orange and black hues clustered around the branches. The combination of autumn leaves and butterflies would have normally been a lovely distraction, but today she had one task in mind: she needed to find Aidan.

AIDAN PULLED AT HIS MANACLES WHILE POWDER FROM THE PEELING WALL fell to mingle with the dirt and blood on the dusty floor. He'd been working the better part of the afternoon and was finally seeing progress. He hoped he'd have a little more time before his captors arrived with another pathetic meal of soggy potatoes and stale bread. His wrists were bruised and bleeding from the continual grinding of metal against flesh. The last visit had been over three hours ago by a timid teenager barely out of high school. The boy had refused to make eye contact or engage in conversation. He appeared exhausted by the look of the dark circles around his eyes. His black cloak hung loosely over his gaunt frame. He put a plate of food and water on the floor close to the shackles. Afterward, the young man scurried outside, bolting the door behind him.

Aidan was starving by this time and had no choice but to accept the meager meal. Without utensils, he was forced to eat with his fingers. Barely able to reach the tray, half of the food ended up on the floor. He imagined the leader enjoyed every ounce of his humiliation. They were intent to keep him alive, as they had for the last few days. *But for what purpose?*

After lunch, he continued to work on his escape attempt. Tiny splinters of plaster crumbled as he gave a final pull. With his right hand liberated, he was able to loosen the rest of the constraints. Once freed, he moved towards the back of the door with chains in hand. He'd be ready for their next visit.

⚜

A RUSTLE OF AUTUMN LEAVES BLEW OVER JADE'S WHITE TENNIS SHOES while she explored the trail. She studied the educational signs set throughout the path. They were instrumental for visitors curious about the monarch migratory patterns and Pacific Grove's long history of hosting them. Normally, she'd take her time reading each one, eager to learn about her newly adopted city, but there wasn't much daylight left, and the trees were ablaze with an orange glow.

She was beginning to wonder if this was a fool's mission when she spotted a blur of ivory feathers out of the corner of her eye.

Jade looked in disbelief at the sight of her raven. Morrigan cawed, setting down on top of a chain link fence adjacent to the trail.

"Morrigan!" she called to her pet, not understanding how she had wound up at the sanctuary. "How did you get here?"

Jade shuddered, suddenly remembering the dream. She put her arm out, hoping Morrigan would come to her. Instead, the raven flew toward a decrepit home on the opposite side of the fence. Her pale blue eyes locked with Jade's gray ones.

Jade left the trail, following her pet. The bird landed on the lawn and hopped toward the front of the house. There were old, faded newspapers covering the windows, torn boards rotting and falling off onto patches of overgrown weeds. A bag of fresh trash was outside the front window. Several rats wiggled over a pile of discarded leftovers.

The fence separating the trail from the abandoned house was over six feet high. Jade followed it until she found a section that was torn. She placed her right foot inside a hole near the middle and pulled herself up over the top. Her feet stung when she landed on the other side, and she cried out in pain.

Moving closer to the window, she peered through a tear in the newspaper. Her mouth fell open in disbelief, seeing Aidan hiding behind a closed door in the back room of the house.

With her heart pounding in her ears, she grabbed her purse, searching frantically for her cellphone.

She shook her head in frustration, realizing her phone was dead.

"Damn it!" she hissed out.

Before she realized what was happening, a hand covered her mouth and she was dragged backward toward the dingy cottage. At the same time Jade stumbled in the darkness, she bit into the meaty palm of her assailant. He hollered in pain, releasing her into the dark hallway. A second man grabbed her by the back of her hoodie, locking her in a chokehold. Her nails clawed his flesh while his fingers tightened around her throat.

An elderly, heavily accented voice sounded behind her. "That's enough, Thomas. Give the lass a bit of air. No need to hurt her."

The bodyguard released his grip and she sucked in her breath.

"Put her inside the room with the creature."

He nodded, unlocking the padlock and pushing her roughly inside. When they entered, Jade noticed Aidan was gone. Her captor grunted and glanced around the musty room.

Aidan leaped from behind the door, wrapping the chain around the man's neck. Thomas fell to his knees. While the man's face turned an alarming shade of purple, Jade was able to jump free. Her eyes narrowed when a second man barreled into the room, his right-hand dripping with blood.

"Aidan!"

He turned in time to see the second guard approaching, released the chain and sent it flying. The attacker immediately fell to the ground, clutching his head in agony. A third man thundered over, grinning with several missing teeth. Aidan punched him in the nose, knocking him to his knees. Blood poured down his face terrifyingly.

"Jade, run!"

She stood frozen, her eyes burning with tears as she watched the men wrestle Aidan to the ground. He glanced toward Jade and said, "Get out of here, lass!"

She had no choice but to obey. When she tried to leave the room, a teenage boy blocked her path.

"Grab her!" the elderly voice called from the shadows.

The young man pinned her by the arms and held her in place. She felt the cold edge of a blade against her throat. Unable to flee, Jade froze in her tracks.

"Drop your weapon or the girl dies."

"Let go of her," Aidan said, dropping his chain to the floor. Thomas scrambled toward him, absently wiping the blood from his mouth. He punched Aidan in the stomach, dropping him to the floor. A second guard came forward with two chairs. The bodyguards pulled Jade and Aidan to their feet, and then forced them to sit back-to-back. The teenager wrapped ropes around their waists, shoulders, and legs, pinning them together. They attached a second set of manacles to the wall securing them to the pair's ankles. They struggled against the restraints in vain. Once they were tied, the leader surveyed the pair with curiosity, his eye lingering on Jade's figure.

"Let's let our lovely couple enjoy their privacy." The men followed their master out of the room, bolting the door behind.

"Lass, are you all right?"

"I'll be fine. Are you hurt?"

"I'll live. How did you find me?"

"I've been so worried about you. After the men attacked us, I ended up in the hospital with a concussion."

"Dear god. A concussion?" He tightened his fists, infuriated by the thought Jade was injured by his captors.

"I'm fine now. I must have hit my head when the men grabbed you. I explained everything that happened to Sheriff Carpenter. He has officers searching for you."

"That's good, darlin'. I just wished you hadn't gotten mixed up in all of this. I can't stand the thought of something else happening to you."

Jade looked around as best as she could, then lowered her voice to a whisper. "I had a dream about this house last night. There were monarch butterflies everywhere. I drove for hours today searching and eventually discovered the Monarch Sanctuary. Morrigan was outside."

Aidan smiled despite their circumstances. "That's incredible detective work, Jade. Have you ever considered a job in law enforcement?"

"No, I think this has been more excitement than my heart can handle."

"I'm sorry, darlin'. We'll find a way out of this mess. I promise. At least now I know our exact location. They blindfolded me on the way over. So, we're near the Sanctuary?"

"Yes, there's an abandoned house adjacent to the trail. I spotted Morrigan outside. I still have no idea why she's here. Once I jumped the fence, I took a closer look. There are newspapers covering every window, but I found a hole to peak through. I could see you inside. I tried to call the station, but my phone was dead. That's when those terrible men grabbed me. I bit one of them, and he let me go."

Aidan chuckled. "Good, lass. I always knew you were a fighter."

"Well, I wasn't successful at my escape attempt. Another man grabbed me. Then a third had a knife at my throat."

"That bastard. God, if I ever get my hands on him…" he said.

"Aidan. I've ruined everything. You might have escaped if I hadn't interfered."

Her lips trembled while tears streaked down her flushed face. She choked back sobs, trying to stifle the sound.

"Aye, it's not your fault, lass. This is all on me. I brought you into this mess. I've been so worried about you the whole time I've been here. Ye nearly drowned the last time I saw you. They wouldn't tell me what happened to you after they dragged me away."

"I'm fine. Sheriff's Carpenter's officers found me unconscious by the cottage. An ambulance took me to the hospital. Mary was there when I woke up. I told Sheriff Carpenter everything that happened."

"Everything that happened?" Aidan echoed.

"Yes, I told him how you saved my life from drowning. I couldn't explain why I was out in the ocean. I still don't understand everything that happened, but I let them know how you saved me. Sheriff Carpenter wanted descriptions of the men, so I told him about our attackers."

"That's all you told them, Jade?"

"That and that you breathed life into me."

"Is that all you remember?"

"Well...not exactly. Your body...it...Did I imagine it, Aidan? Please, I'm desperate to understand."

Aidan closed his eyes taking a deep breath. "Yes, it's true, I'm afraid. My family's ancestors were Selkie Folk. I'm what's known as a half-breed, though I'm more like an eighth. It's why I can go back and forth between the two worlds, though not as easily as a true selkie. So, yes, the tales are true."

Jade considered this, trying to understand. She didn't realize how long the silence had stretched until it was broken.

"Do you think me a monster?"

Jade shook her head back and forth, yearning to hold him. "I don't care what you call yourself. You mean the world to me." She strained against the restraints, trying to free herself from the chains. Tears slid down her cheeks and her body trembled, shaking her chair and Aidan's.

"Please don't cry, lass. We'll find a way out of this. They took me, not you, so there must be something they need of me."

Jade nodded. "It was so terrifying to wake up and not know what happened to you. Do you know anything about these men, Aidan? What do they want from you?"

He took a deep breath and let it out slowly. "I suspect they belong to the same cult that's been stalking my family all these years. Their leader knows about my...condition. I'm not exactly sure what they have planned, but I expect it's not going to be pleasant."

"Oh, god. So, the tales are true? There's an ancient cult intent on destroying Selkie Folk? Wait, they're called the Hunters, right? There's a Hunter's Moon tomorrow. They've been talking about it on the news. It's supposed to be unusually bright and orange. That can't be insignificant."

"You're probably right. The man in charge is particularly obsessed with his mission. I suspect there might be something personal in it for him. My family lost its lore of magic when they immigrated; there had been enough bad tales of magic in America and my great-grandmother just wanted to make sure her family was safe."

"Aidan, what I don't understand is that if The Hunters are for you…why did they target my home and not yours? Was the seal pelt left for you or me?"

"The first one I suspect was a simple warning. Our families have been connected in the past, so they may have thought you knew about me. The second time…I suspect they've been watching us. They must have picked up on the fact you're important to me."

"So, I was the bait," Jade said.

Aidan nodded. "Appears that way."

"Then it is my fault."

"You're a true Catholic, lass."

"What are you talking about?"

"You feel guilty for everything," he chuckled.

Jade smiled weakly, amazed he could still laugh despite their dire circumstances.

"We both made choices. I believe this was doomed to happen one way or another. We need to figure out how to escape," Aidan said.

"The Hunter's Moon rises tomorrow. If they're planning something, it might happen then."

"I know, lass. I mentioned before, the station's always busy during full moons. It affects people. I've always made a point to keep note of the lunar cycles. It helps me prepare for work."

Jade nodded. "That makes sense. I've been trying to figure out clues since you've been gone. Mary and I continued our research this week. Madame Garnier visited the shop yesterday. She asked to do a reading for me. I agreed. She sensed I needed answers. So, I went to her house."

"You visited a psychic?" Aidan said skeptically.

"I was desperate, Aidan. It's been days and no one could find you. I figured it couldn't hurt."

Aidan nodded. "I'm not judging, lass. I appreciate your concern for me. I'm just surprised since you mentioned she frightened you during the grand opening."

"She did, but I took a chance anyway. She gave me a Tarot card reading. Madame Garnier suggested I was intuitive and encouraged me to trust my hunches. Thought it might be a good idea to purchase a journal to write down my dreams. That's exactly what I did this morning and then the monarch butterflies and they led me to you."

"You're a rare woman, Jade. I'm glad you trusted your instinct. Things are not always what they appear."

For the next several hours they discussed plans for their escape. Shadows spread throughout the room while the sun set. The couple leaned back in their chairs and they prepared for their first night together in prison.

Chapter Nineteen

MARY PUSHED BACK A LOCK OF BRUNETTE HAIR BEHIND HER EAR, SEARCHING the road in vain. She and Deputy Rheinstein had been driving for hours. The fog had yet to lift and night had truly set it. Mary refused to admit that the likelihood of finding Jade or Aidan tonight was slim.

"If only I'd gotten out of bed when I heard Dougal crying this morning, I might have prevented Jade from leaving," Mary said, shaking her head back and forth in frustration.

"How could you have known?" Deputy Rheinstein asked.

Mary ignored the question, focusing her attention on the colorful leaves dancing across the sidewalks.

"And if that's not bad enough, her poor bird escaped. Morrigan flew out the door when I let Dougal out to potty. Jade will be heartbroken when she finds out. Do you suppose those cloaked men found her?" Mary didn't give the deputy a chance to answer. She was too upset to listen.

"Jade described their attack on the beach. They sounded just awful. I can't bear the thought." She bit down hard on her lower lip, trying desperately to keep it together.

The officer beside her scanned the road and alleyways along Lighthouse Avenue while she brooded.

"We've been looking for hours, Miss Deane. It might be a good idea to go back home and sleep on it. Maybe tomorrow morning you'll have some fresh ideas?"

Mary stroked Dougal's head while he snuggled on her lap.

"I guess you're right. I should probably get this poor dog back to the house and feed him some dinner. I really appreciate your help today."

"My pleasure. Hopefully, we'll find something out tomorrow. The search will continue tonight with more patrol units. We also have a car stationed by the cottage."

"Thank you. It's good to know there's officers working the case. Just let me know if I can help in any way."

"Appreciate it."

Deputy Rheinstein pulled the cruiser into the parking lot behind the police station. After he'd parked, he rushed to her side to open the door. Mary led Dougal out on his leash and grabbed her purse. The dog sniffed the concrete with interest. The deputy reached into his pocket and pulled out his business card from his wallet.

"If you think of anything, just call night or day. I'll check back with you tomorrow. Try to get some rest." It seemed to Mary that his green eyes lingered on her face just a little longer than necessary. "Just remember Sheriff Carpenter's organizing a second group to search this evening. So, there's no use of you not getting a good night's sleep and being ready in the morning."

She nodded, knowing she wouldn't rest until her friend was back home safe and sound.

"Thank you for everything. It's a relief to know there's extra patrol cars out."

"Are you sure you're comfortable going back to the cottage alone?"

"Yes, I want to be there if Morrigan comes back. I'll make sure to set the alarm. Jade gave me the code last night."

"Morrigan...the white raven?" His eyebrows rose in question.

She let out her breath. "Yes, it turns out I'm the worst pet sitter in the word. I just hope she knows her way back to the house."

The officer was a quiet a moment, studying her face with a lingering smile.

"It was nice spending the day together, Miss Deane. I wish it were under better circumstances."

"Deputy Rheinstein, I can't thank you enough. And please, call me Mary."

"Only if you'll call me Paul," he said with a smile.

Mary looked up into his green eyes and smiled. The officer was over a foot taller than her. His chiseled features made for an exceptionally handsome face. If she wasn't so worried about her friend, she would have noticed his beautiful smile earlier. Normally, she would have been distracted by a man this attractive the entire car ride.

"Thank you, Paul."

"Don't forget to call if you need anything…day or night."

"Will do."

Mary made her way over to her car and let herself in.

The fog was thick, making it difficult to see as she drove down the private road towards Jade's cottage. She switched on her low beams, squinting in the dark. Mary parked outside and let Dougal out on his leash. He sniffed the ground, lingering a moment by the front door.

Once inside the gate, she let him off leash to do his business.

She scanned the beach, searching for Morrigan. It was difficult to see anything in the thick fog.

"Morrigan?" she called.

She waited for several minutes, calling repeatedly, hoping for any sign of Jade or the raven. After listening to the roar of the waves a moment, she retrieved her keychain. The security system beeped when she entered, so she punched in the code. Once she activated the alarm, she made her way into the kitchen. Dougal followed. His fuzzy tail thumped against the hardwood floors anticipating dinner. She prepared his bowl of kibble and topped it off with his favorite canned dog food. She wriggled her nose at the pungent aroma.

"There you go, buddy."

Dougal immediately began lapping up his supper.

She glanced over at Morrigan's perch, overwhelmed with guilt. She said a prayer the bird would come back to the cottage. After she changed into pajamas, she made a salad and took a seat at the kitchen table. It felt strange being in her friend's cottage alone, and she wanted to do everything in her power to bring her home.

She reached for Mary's note inside her purse and re-read the page three more times.

"Where did you go, Jade?" she asked the empty cottage. "Why were you looking for butterflies?"

The note implied a connection to Aidan's disappearance. Jade was looking for clues related to another dream. Mary would have laughed at the idea a few months ago, but now, with everything that had taken place, she couldn't take anything for granted. She walked beneath the fireplace mantel and shook her head. The changes in the painting were beyond rational. It frustrated her. There was always a logical answer if you looked hard and long enough. She tapped her manicured nails on the kitchen table, trying to put together the clues so far.

After dinner, she powered up her laptop and researched articles on Monterey and butterflies. She found that Pacific Grove was famous for their migration of monarchs that arrived every October. The town was even nicknamed "Butterfly Town, U.S.A." The Monarch Grove Sanctuary was close to town and run by volunteers. Even the Police Department was involved in protecting the colorful butterflies. She was surprised to learn there were laws in place against interfering or disturbing them. A fine of one thousand dollars was enforced for anyone caught harming the insects.

Her eyes widened as she scrolled further down the page. According to the article, thousands of monarchs were being tracked via butterfly watchers and were due to arrive as early as next week to overwinter in Pacific Grove's Sanctuary on the pine, cypress, and eucalyptus trees that were being preserved for them. She stretched her fingers over the table. Had they already arrived? If so, what did this mean to her investigation?

Mary leaned forward in her chair. The article was dated October 9th, so the timing was right. It seemed like such a long shot, but it was all she had to work with. The sanctuary was located on Saint Ridge Road, about a block from Lighthouse Avenue according to the article.

She spent the next two hours reading everything she could find concerning their migration patterns. Mary examined a map of Pacific grove, hoping to familiarize herself with area. Hopefully, these clues might lead her to her friend's whereabouts. It was past midnight when she finally drifted into a restless sleep.

Her dreams were full of fire, white ravens, and screams.

Chapter Twenty

Sunlight penetrated through a tiny opening in the newspaper covered window. Aidan and Jade glanced up while the door creaked open. Two oversized bodyguards followed a cloaked figure into the room. The pair waited quietly with food trays gripped in their meaty hands.

The leader reached gnarled fingers toward Jade's face, pushing back a sandy-blond curl from her forehead. She shuddered and backed away from his icy touch.

"Stay away from her, she has nothing to do with us," Aidan hissed.

"Silence, creature. Lass, do you not understand you've been keeping company with the unholy?"

He moved closer when she refused to answer. "Perhaps you need to undergo a purification ritual." His good eye lingered on her curves and the right corner of his mouth twitched.

"The only unholy person is you. You have no right to keep us here. Let us go," Jade growled.

"So brave and reckless," the leader chuckled while his gaze traveled over her body. "Your manners are need of improvement. Yes, I believe schooling is in order. You will soon learn to act like a proper woman."

Aidan struggled in his chains as the man stood over Jade. He opened his hand toward her chin. Yellowed nails slipped over her delicate flesh, forcing her to look up at his face. She recoiled at his touch, attempting to back away.

Aidan struggled against his restraints. "Leave her alone, ye scabby bastard!"

The leader gestured towards his bodyguard. Thomas grinned with a mouthful of missing teeth as he back-handed Aidan across the face. Blood trickled from Aidan's mouth and nose, but he still glared at the men.

"Aidan!"

The leader reached for the hood of his cloak, pushing it away absently. Jade recoiled from the sight. Half of his flesh was a scarred mass of ancient wounds. His left eye socket was hollow, while his right eye looked inhuman, like an opal—white and glistening.

"Does my face frighten you, child?"

She stared in horror at the grizzly terrain of open gashes and scars.

"You'll grow accustomed. There will be plenty of time to become acquainted after the ceremony." He covered his head with the cloak and his guards followed behind him like obedient hounds.

The door closed with a sharp click and was bolted shut.

Jade shuddered at the thought of the man's ice-cold fingers on her skin.

Aidan groaned and his head fell forward. Drops of blood spilled over his bottom lip.

"Aidan!" Jade cried.

"Jade..." He shook his head, trying to focus.

"Are you alright? You're going to get a concussion if they keep hitting you in the head."

"I'll be fine. I've had beams collapse on my head. It's you I'm worried about. I'm just...I don't know what to do. You need to get out of here. I can't let that man touch you again."

"We're going to get out of this mess, lass. I promise you."

Jade smiled weakly, trying to put her thoughts together. She knew nothing good could come by panicking. There had to be a way to escape. Unfortunately, her sudden appearance robbed Aidan's of his chance. If only she'd arrived a little while afterward. She shook her head, trying to keep her voice level so he wouldn't tell how terrified she felt.

"We just have today to figure a way out of here, Aidan. Maybe Mary will come up with something. I left her a letter and imagine she's been to the Sheriff by now. She's probably in a state after I failed to return to the cottage. I just wish I knew why Morrigan escaped. Hopefully, they're both safe."

"Does she know…everything?" Aidan was quiet, waiting for her answer.

"I did tell her what I witnessed…the metamorphosis. She also noticed the changes in the portrait at my house. Mary's a logical person. She places a lot of importance on the facts and figures. Most likely researching while we speak. Your secret is safe."

"Aidan?" Jade asked. "If we get out of this…will you leave because I know your secret?"

"Oh, lass," Aidan groaned, "I've been trying to keep my distance since the day we met, knowing what I was, but I couldn't stay away. It's the reason things stayed platonic for as long as they have between us. I've wanted you so badly. Not sure what would have happened if the sheriff hadn't interrupted on the couch. God, it's been agony for me knowing you're alone in your bedroom. It's taken every ounce of strength to stay away from ye, lass. So no, I won't be leaving after this. Far from that. If you'll be amenable to it, that is."

Jade sighed, relieved to know she wasn't the only one suffering from their situation.

"Aidan, I feel the same way. I wondered why you never made another move. To be honest, I really don't know what would have happened if we hadn't been interrupted. It's just…I've never done that before."

Aidan's sucked in his breath, his eyes widening in the dark room.

"Jade, I thought…didn't you say you had a boyfriend before we met? You mentioned it in the sheriff's office the day he questioned you about the seal pelt."

Jade's face turned crimson. She didn't really want to discuss this, but she was pleased that even then, he'd been listening for clues about her love life. She was silent for a few minutes as she found the right words.

"I had a boyfriend in grad school. We never…consummated our relationship. It just never seemed right. In the beginning, I tried to convince myself I loved him, but my feelings were not genuine. I broke things off a few weeks before graduation, shortly before my mom passed away."

"Darlin', I had no idea. God, lass. You have nothing to worry about. I'll show you what real love is like. It's good the sheriff came by, then, though. I don't know how delicate I would have been. I've been wanting you for months and just being in your house while you were naked in the shower was difficult enough for me. I tried…I wanted to keep things casual until the suspects were apprehended."

"And then what?"

He was quiet for a moment trying to collect his thoughts. "I was going to give you some space. I didn't know how to explain my true nature."

Her face flushed. "You were going to just leave me?"

"It's what I told myself, but it was a lie, if I'm going to be honest."

"Why? What changed your mind?"

"I'm in love with you."

Jade's breath hitched in her throat; her gray eyes brimmed with tears. She released her breath with an audible sigh.

"I love you, too."

He bit down on his lower lip and shook his head. "How can you love me knowing what I truly am?"

"It doesn't matter to me. All I know is how I feel. I nearly lost my mind with worry since you've been gone. Last night, I had the most horrific nightmare. Men with black hoods dragged you across a moonlit shore. Aidan, they had a knife…and…" her voice shook, and she found there were no words to describe what she witnessed. The image was unspeakable. "I was too far away to stop them." Jade's voice was barely above a whisper. "It worries me that my dreams are beginning to overlap with my waking life. There's no way I would have found you, if it weren't for seeing the butterflies in my dream. I followed a swarm of Monarchs to the Sanctuary this afternoon. Morrigan was outside the house like I imagined she would be. What if these dreams are glimpses of the future?" she said, struggling against her constraints.

"I don't know the magic of my ancestors, lass. But I'd guess that you have second sight, love. I just hope what you imagined happening to me on the beach doesn't come to fruition."

Jade gasped. Was it possible that she had magic too? Her mind raced.

"Let's just focus on trying to get out of this mess, love. Together, we'll figure something out," Aidan said.

Jaded nodded. "Alright, let's start from the beginning. How are we going to get out of these chairs?"

The couple began their plan of escape while a beam of bright sunlight began its trek across the room.

Chapter Twenty-One

THE LATE-MORNING SUN STREAMED THROUGH THE NEWSPAPER-COVERED windows. Aidan had fallen asleep after their conversation and though Jade had tried to keep him up in case he had a concussion, he was currently asleep. Jade winced from the sharp tingling sensations in her bound arms and legs.

The door creaked open a few inches, letting in a cold draft along with a stream of light. By the sudden movement, Aidan was now awake. A teenage boy appeared with a tray of potatoes and bread. He glanced at Jade, and then quickly looked down at the floor. Aidan's fists clenched when he approached with their meals.

"I brought ye some breakfast. Sorry…it's not much," he said quietly in a mild Scottish accent.

Jade recognized him from her capture the day before. He had seemed sympathetic. She might even be able to convince him to help them. She batted her long lashes, flashing a friendly smile.

"Thank you. I'm Jade and this is my friend Aidan. What's your name?" She gazed upwards, her steel-gray eyes searching his face.

"I'm really not supposed to say."

He glanced over his shoulder, and then placed the tray by her feet.

"You don't belong with them," Aidan said with sudden. "Do you want out?"

He shrugged. "I don't have anywhere else to go."

"Are you from Scotland, lad?" Aidan asked.

"Yep."

"Please, tell me your name," Jade said. "Maybe we can help you. Things are different in America, you know."

He looked back over his shoulder, then seeing they were alone moved closer.

"It's Finnean."

She smiled, flashing pearly white teeth. "Finnean, it's nice to meet you."

He shook his head, staring down at the dirty floor. "Nice to meet ye."

"I hear Scotland is a lovely country. I've always wanted to go abroad. Do you like it there, Finnean?"

"I guess it's a good a place as any." He shrugged. "It's all the same I suppose."

Aidan bit the inside of his lip wondering what Jade was up to.

"They told me since yer hands are bound, I should try to feed ye," Finnean said.

"I'm afraid I'm not hungry. This has all been a terrible shock for me," Jade said with a sigh.

Finnean looked uncomfortable.

"Sorry, miss. I wish I could help ye. The thing is…they'll whip me if ye refuse the meal. I don' think I can bear another lashing."

Jade's eyes widened in surprise. "I'm so sorry. That's terrible. I'll try a few bites. Why don't you come closer?"

The teenager brought the tray over to Jade, looking uncertain.

"Do ye want some potatoes or bread first?" Finnean asked.

"Either would be fine."

With a trembling hand, he lifted a forkful of soggy potatoes to her mouth. She took a bite, wrinkling her nose in response to the moldy flavor.

"I don't suppose you have any coffee?"

"Sorry." He shook his head, looking at the floor. "I wish I had something better to offer. It's all we eat these days."

"That's a shame. You don't deserve to be treated so poorly. You're still growing, but I can't imagine stale, bland food will help you get stronger." She looked up at the teenager's face and smiled.

"I'm sure my friend Aidan would like some breakfast, too."

He nodded, moving the tray to him. The firefighter accepted the food in silence, throwing Jade looks as he ate.

"Do you have any pets, Finnean? I have one at home. My friends have been taking care of her for me, but they are probably looking for me right now. I'm so worried about them."

Finnean moved towards the door, making sure no one was nearby.

"What kind of pets do ye got?"

"I have a white raven named Morrigan and Aidan has an adorable Scottie."

"A white raven?" He pushed his fingers through his greasy hair. "Lady, that's seriously metal!" he said with an admiring glance.

"Thank you," Jade said graciously, though she wasn't sure what he meant.

"Finnean, my friend and I haven't done anything wrong. We just want to go home. Could you help us?" she pleaded

His mouth drew down in a tight line.

"Lady…I can't."

"Please call me Jade."

"Miss Jade, ye might be innocent, but yer friend's an abomination."

Jade heard Aidan take a deep, shaky breath, probably to control his temper, but she kept her eyes on the boy

"No, I assure you he's not. He's a fireman and a good person. He risks his own life to save others every day. You've been told lies."

"It's true, lad," Aidan said. "I have friends at the sheriff's office. I can tell them you had nothing to do with this mess…if you can get us out. You have my word."

The teenager licked at his bottom lip, then ran his fingers through his hair.

Footsteps echoed down the hall while he glanced between them.

"I gotta go."

He hurried out the room with their leftovers. They listened to the door lock behind him.

Aidan smiled in admiration of Jade's performance. "That was pretty good, lass."

"He looked like he was going to bite for a minute," she said.

"I thought so too."

"We need to get out of here. The Hunter's Moon's rising tonight." Her eyes filled with tears. "I can't bear the thought of those horrible men hurting you."

"We'll find a way, lass. I give you my word."

❦

MARY SAT UP IN BED, RUNNING HER FINGERS THROUGH HER SMOOTH TRESSES. Dougal jumped onto the couch and licked her face.

"It's alright, boy." She stepped into her slippers and padded to the kitchen to fill his bowl.

Mary spent the morning driving around Pacific Grove trying to find traces of her friends' whereabouts. Afterward, she walked along the beach calling Morrigan's name. There were no signs of the bird or her friend. By noon, the sky darkened over the ocean, bringing heavy rains. She hurried inside the cottage to escape the downpour. A few hours later there was a knock on the front door. Deputy Rheinstein was waiting outside with hat in hand. He offered his boyish smile while she opened the door.

"Afternoon, Mary. I thought you might like to join me on patrol duty while there's a break in the weather."

"That would be perfect! Do you mind if I bring Dougal?"

The deputy grinned, giving the terrier a pat on the head. "The little guy is welcome to join us."

"Great. Come on inside. I'll grab Dougal's leash and my coat."

A few minutes later, Mary and Deputy Rheinstein were combing the streets of Pacific Grove. They drove for nearly two hours while discussing the case. Mary glanced over at the deputy as he scanned the road. "I know this is a crazy hunch, but could we check out the Monarch Sanctuary?"

His eyebrows rose in question. "Sure."

They drove down Saint Ridge Road, parking the cruiser in the Sanctuary's empty parking lot and made their way along the eucalyptus-lined trail. Monarchs covered the trees in shrouds of orange and black velvet. The contrast with the setting sun was breathtaking. An orange glow slipped through the branches of the trees, illuminating the path. Shadows followed their footsteps and they explored the Sanctuary.

"We'll be losing daylight pretty soon," Paul said.

"Yes, I don't even know why I stopped here…just a hunch." Mary's eyes widened in disbelief.

"Oh, my god!"

Adjacent to the walkway was a fence separating a row of abandoned houses.

A white raven perched on top of the nearest one.

"It's Morrigan," she whispered.

"Who?"

"Jade's raven!"

Mary ran to the fence, realizing there was no way to go around it. Throwing caution to the wind, she slipped her sneaker inside a hole in the fence and lifted herself upward.

The deputy's eyes widened when she proceeded to climb to the top. He rushed after her, a mere step behind.

"Be careful, Mary. We don't know what might be waiting for us in there!"

She nodded, gracefully landing on the other side. He gave her an admiring smile, pulling himself over the chain link fence. "Still, running into danger, you'd be a natural at the academy," he said. "Please, though, stay behind me now."

"Thanks. I think I'll stick to running my gallery." She laughed, shaking her head at the thought of working for the police department.

Mary squinted at the row of houses, searching for Morrigan.

"Here, I brought a flashlight from the car." Officer Rheinstein led the way, pointing the light toward the abandoned building in front of them.

Mary noticed a flash of pearly feathers near the front door of an abandoned house. "Morrigan!"

The movement drew their attention to the tattered newspaper covering the windows. They looked at each other worriedly. Morrigan flew toward the roof and cawed. The deputy shook his head, listening to the chorus of crickets hidden in the weeds.

"Mary, something's not right. I need you to stay here while I look."

"Alright. Please be careful, Paul."

The officer drew his pistol, moving toward the front door.

He pounded on the wooded barrier. "Pacific Grove Police Department! Is anyone inside?" When no one answered he kicked the door open.

Mary waited outside wringing her hands together. When the deputy failed to return, she decided to take matters into her own hands. She clicked the flashlight on her phone and followed him inside. Deputy Rheinstein had his gun out. His eyes widened when he noticed Mary behind him. "I don't want to frighten you, but it appears someone was being held against their will. There are chains and ropes in the bedroom," he whispered.

She quickly took in the scene, noticing bags of garbage strewn across the living room and kitchen. An oversized rat was feasting on leftover potatoes piled over an old card table. The rodent's eyes glowed red when the officer's flashlight exposed his hiding place. It leapt from its meal and went scurrying over the warped floorboards, disappearing into the darkness. She followed the deputy into the empty bedroom, eyes widening when she spotted two chairs chained together, along with a pile of discarded manacles strewn across the floor.

"Oh my god. Do you think Aidan and Jade were held prisoner here?"

"It's possible. Stay back while I check the rest of the house."

"Paul, look!" Mary said pointing toward the ground.

The deputy's mouth pinched together when he noticed a single white Keds sneaker on the floor by the front door.

"That looks like Jade's shoe," Mary said. The raven cawed from the front yard. They followed the sound, through the house, exiting to see the bird disappearing into a blanket of mist.

"Morrigan!"

She ran down the sidewalk, waving her hands. Deputy Rheinstein followed. Mary stopped at the crosswalk waiting for the light to turn green, turning toward the officer with wide eyes. "I think Morrigan knows where they've gone."

"You think the bird knows?" Paul asked skeptically. The deputy ran his hand over the back of his crewcut. "Dogs, yes. Cats, maybe. Birds don't do what Lassie does, Mary."

"I know how it sounds...but Morrigan led us to the abandoned house. Maybe she knows which direction they've gone."

The officer considered Mary's earnest eyes and sighed. "Alright, the station has a history of using psychics in the past. What's the worst thing that could happen by following a white raven around town? I'll end up spending my evening with a lovely young lady beneath the Hunter's Moon."

Mary blushed at the compliment and smiled. "Thank you."

He put his arm out and she took it, amazed there were still a few gentlemen left in the world.

"Shall we?"

"We shall," she said.

"I'll radio in about the abandoned house and ask for backup. They can continue processing the scene. Let's walk back to the car."

Mary's heart pounded, hoping they were onto something. Once inside the patrol unit, she fidgeted with her seatbelt while Deputy Rheinstein called for dispatch. He reported the address of the abandoned house and gave a detailed description of the scene. The deputy ended the call by explaining they were in pursuit of a lead and would be in contact shortly. After he'd finished, he turned to Mary with a smile. "Alright, let's do this."

She leaned forward while the deputy maneuvered the cruiser toward Lighthouse Avenue.

"Oh, look! Morrigan's perched in that tree with the colorful lanterns." Mary said, pointing toward the intersection.

Paul squinted in the haze, watching the raven flapping her ivory wings in the fading light.

"You're right. It's crazy, but it appears she's waiting for us. I'll be."

Once they drew up alongside the lanterned tree, Morrigan took to the sky and headed toward the seaside.

Dougal crawled from the backseat and curled up on Mary's lap. "Let's go find our friends."

Chapter Twenty-Two

JADE SHIVERED WHILE HER SPLAYED FINGERS SEARCHED THE AIR. SHE couldn't see a thing and wondered what Aidan was feeling in this moment. A sharp poke in the back pushed her forward.

"I'm going, just give me a moment," she said.

"Leave her alone," Aidan hissed between his teeth. Jade whimpered, hearing the fury in his voice. She knew he was furious that she'd gotten pulled into this, but she was still happy to have been there for him. They'd both been blindfolded and brought outside into the stinging rain and led to an unknown vehicle. Neither of them knew what was in store for them. The possibilities were terrifying. They were dealing with desperate men with an agenda spanning centuries.

Jade figured their only chance was to find a way to get through to Finnean. If he felt uncertain about the situation, perhaps he might take pity on them and help them escape. While her thoughts turned to the rest of the men, she considered the leader's deformed face and shuddered. He appeared to have an unhealthy interest concerning her and her relationship with Aidan. The idea chilled her to the bone.

"Where are we going?" Aidan asked.

"Shut up, or I'll shut you up!"

Jade recognized the voice of the leader's bodyguard, Thomas. He frightened her almost as the old man. Jade stumbled over the sandy beach, listening to the waves hit the shore. When she breathed in the ocean air, a feeling of homesickness swept over her. She wanted nothing more than to go back to her cottage with Aidan. They'd only spent a small time together, but she only wanted more. He'd become so safe and comforting that she was already finding herself considering him like family.

A biting wind nipped her cheeks as she limped across the damp sand. She'd lost her shoe in the struggle to the car. Wet sand filled the remaining Keds shoe and sock, irritating her chilled skin. Rough hands grabbed her shoulders, pushing her down toward the damp earth. Aidan was forced down next to her. He leaned against Jade, trying his best to comfort her.

They sat for almost an hour together, shivering as they felt the warmth of the sun fade behind them until there was only the cool night wind.

They breathed in the aroma of burning driftwood as the men prepared a bonfire. The warmth was a welcome sensation and brought back happier times of youth, which jarred considerably with their current situations. The wind shifted and Jade began to cough when the smoke filled her nose.

"Are you alright, lass?"

"Be silent, creature." Jade heard a grunt when Thomas kicked his prisoner in the back.

"Aidan!" she whispered, unsure of where the men were.

As she listened to him struggle, Jade found herself being pulled to her feet and dragged, stumbling closer to the fire.

"It's time for the ceremony," the elderly leader announced. "Take the blindfolds off of our guests."

Jade blinked in the sudden, flickering light of the fire and saw Aidan doing the same out of the corner of her eye. She tried to make sense of where she was. Stars danced across the sky as the Hunter's Moon illuminated the beach. Jade glanced over her shoulder, noticing the familiar tidepools. She shuddered, realizing they were close to her cottage. She whispered a silent prayer, hoping the patrol officers spotted them. The bodyguards set metal rods across the open flames of the pyre. Jade's eyes widened watching the men secure poles deep into the wet sand, remembering what the sheriff had said about that second bonfire they had found.

"What are they doing," she whispered.

"I don't know, love. They need me. To accomplish their goals...of eradication." Jade gasped, recognizing the metal rods and frame now as a cooking rack. She heaved, feeling sick.

"Jade," Aidan whispered fervently, "you need to try to get out of here. I'll stall them for all I'm worth to give ye time, but you'd best forget about me. Please, it's hard enough knowing that ye've come to danger because of me, please don't make it worse. Don't watch."

Jade searched his face, sensing what it cost him to speak. He looked white and nauseated, but also determined. The leader came forward, slipping his hood from his head. His pearly right eye shone in the moonlight. A gnarled hand reached beneath his cloak as he retrieved a serrated knife. A flash of metal shone beneath the light of the orange moon.

He stood before Aidan smiling. "It's almost time, creature."

"Go to Hell," Aidan said.

"You'll be there soon enough, creature, though I will be welcomed beside the Lord for ridding his world of tainted demon-spawn."

His bodyguards surrounded Aidan, yanking him toward the bonfire. Jade screamed and struggled as their leader approached. Thomas came forward, holding her painfully by the arms.

"Let go of her," Aidan said. He lunged forward when the jagged edge of the knife wielded above her head.

"Jade!"

The leader cut a lock of her curls while another man punched Aidan in the kidneys. He fell to his knees in agony. Jade was thrown to the ground and her hair passed around the circle that had formed around the fire.

"Aidan!" Jade crawled towards him on her knees with her hands tied behind her back

The men gathered around the flames began to chant in Latin. Their voices had a familiar hum and Jade realized with horror that the whispers she'd heard back at the cottage were the same chanting of her captors. She shivered knowing they'd been practicing their dark rituals outside her home. When their voices rose to a crescendo, the leader tossed the golden strands into the fire.

Blue light exploded when the flames consumed the sandy-blond lock. Thomas pulled Jade to her feet and presented her to his master. The leader's gnarled fingers caressed her waist as he leaned close to her ear.

"I hope you said your goodbyes, lass. You belong to me now. You will learn to obey without question. Behold the consequences for those I disfavor." He turned his attention to Finnean. "Remove your cloak."

The teenager looked aghast being asked to undress.

"I won't ask again. Remove it."

The boy stripped off his clothes and stood bare, trembling beneath the inky sky.

"Turn around," the leader said.

Jade gasped at the open sores and whip marks crisscrossing his emaciated body.

"This is what happens when you don't obey your master. It would be a pity to have to damage your lovely flesh."

She pulled away, her mouth quivering. "You're a monster."

"We shall see."

His twisted fingers stroked over her golden tresses, pulling her tightly against his body. The bodyguards grabbed Aidan to his feet to bound him with ropes. He struggled when they attempted to secure his legs. He head-butted Thomas, and then turned to face the others. The men gathered in a tight circle, closing in on him.

Without the use of his hands, his chances were slim. He pulled free of his ankle constraints and kicked one of the bodyguards in the face. When he collapsed, his partner came forward. Aidan kicked the new assailant in the jaw, sending a spray of blood across the sand. Finnean stood with his mouth ajar, eyes wide with shock. His master tightened his grip on Jade, glaring at the boy.

"You coward! Take him now!"

Finnean backed away from the scene, eyes wide with fear.

"You will regret your disobedience, lad. You'll be begging for death once I'm through with you," he growled

The leader turned his attention back to Jade, placing a jagged blade to her throat.

"Creature, surrender or the lass dies."

"Run, Aidan!" Jade trembled while the leader held the knife to her throat. When he pushed the edge closer, trickles of blood surfaced across her smooth skin. She screamed in terror as he applied more pressure.

"Let her be!" Aidan said, falling to his knees.

The bodyguards tackled him to the ground, pummeling him with their fists and boots. Thomas wrapped a thick rope around his neck and led him over to his master.

The leader removed the blade from Jade's throat but kept his hand on her waist. She knew that she would be brought down if she tried to run. She trembled helplessly as she watched the men pull Aidan toward the fire.

"You will pay for your disobedience, creature," the man said to Aidan. "Behold!" he announced to his followers. "Behold the cursed half-breed. Its demon-begotten seal pelt dissolves upon the ground, so we must adapt the ceremony for the glory of God's purity! We'll start with your feet instead. The holy flames will consume your human flesh while your selkie half burns underneath." He heaved a breath, then whispered, "It's a shame, really. I would have enjoyed watching it burn. So, we've made some special changes for today's ceremony. It will take much longer to die, but this is your fate. This is your choice."

Aidan's jaw tightened and he tried to pull free from the rope around his neck.

Jade fell to the ground turning toward her captor in despair. "No, please. Let him go! I'm begging you."

He chuckled, watching her grovel. "That's a good lass. You belong on your knees before a man, eager to serve him however you can with your pathetic life."

The leader turned his attention to Finnean. The right side of his mouth twitched while studying him.

"The boy has proven to be a coward and traitor."

Thomas grabbed him by the throat, pushing him down to his master's feet. Finnean glared, rage burning in his veins.

"So, you think you've found your courage, lad? We'll see how brave you are when your flesh is melting from your bones."

Finnean struggled while the guards hog-tied his feet and hands. "Please, have mercy!"

Thomas punched him in the side of the head, knocking him backward.

"The time has come to do God's glory. Let us begin," the leader said.

DEPUTY RHEINSTEIN AND MARY FOLLOWED MORRIGAN FOR SEVERAL MILES, following the shoreline leading toward Jade's cottage.

"Paul, do you suppose the men in cloaks are near the cottage?" Mary said.

"I can't say for sure. Maybe the raven is just going back to a familiar place like a homing pigeon," the officer said.

They watched Morrigan disappear behind the hillside. Mary's eyes widened when she noticed a patch of ice plants covering the steep side of the road. The colorful flowers glowed orange beneath the rays of the Hunter's Moon.

"The tide pools!" Mary said.

"What tide pools?" The Deputy glanced at Mary in confusion.

"There's a cove by Jade's house. It's a sheltered area covered in ice plants. There're tide pools underneath. You can't see it from the road. Morrigan is headed in that direction. I think that's where they are!"

"Are you sure?"

"It has to be."

"I'm calling in for backup."

After a quick briefing, the deputy turned to Mary and explained how the detectives were combing through the abandoned house looking for clues and dusting for fingerprints. Sheriff Carpenter was on his way to the cove with several officers.

"How long will it take? I can't stand by and wait forever. My friends are in danger." She started down the hillside, bracing against the wind.

"Mary, it's not safe! Please wait for backup."

"I'm just going to look!"

Paul hurried after her as she descended over the sandy hill, stopping her just before the bluff. They knelt on the ground studying the flames of the bonfire.

Deputy Rheinstein reached for her hand, gesturing her to be quiet.

"They're down there, Paul. I can see them." She shivered, her eyes filling with tears.

"I know, but we can't approach until we're ready. They outnumber us, and without backup, most will get away," he said.

"It looks like they're getting ready to do something. Aidan's tied up by the fire. I can see Jade off to the side. I can't just stand and watch my friends get killed."

"I know it's difficult, but we can't let them know we're here. Just wait a few more minutes."

"And do what?"

"Nothing. You're untrained, unarmed, and a liability. The officers will arrive soon. There are several patrol units on the way. We have the advantage of surprise right now. If there's imminent danger, I'll go down by myself. I promise I'll do everything in my power to help your friends. Do you trust me?"

She glanced up and sighed. "Yes, I trust you." Paul gazed into her dark brown eyes and moved closer. "Everything's going to be alright."

She nodded, grateful for his help. I believe you, Paul."

He took her elbow and smiled. "Good. Let's step back from the ledge and move behind those boulders." He pointed to a rocky outcropping a few yards down the cliff. "This way we'll be able to watch without being seen. Once they were hidden from view, they turned their attention back to the shore with their hands clasped tightly, holding their breath waiting for backup.

✧

THE LEADER CHANTED OVER THE BONFIRE. WHILE HE RECITED HIS ancestors' incantations, his mind drifted to the days of his youth. He'd learned from an early age what it meant to belong to the family of Hunters. As a boy, he'd learned from the time he could walk that the Selkie Folk were to be both feared and loathed. His father never missed an opportunity to instill discipline in his continuing education. Mercy had no place in his upbringing. His father explained there was only one way to enter God's kingdom. This was through sacrifice and obedience. At his eighteenth birthday, he learned for the last time that mercy had no place for women or selkies when his father had captured a selkie woman for him as a gift to earn his own place in God's glory and rid the world of the abomination as a man. He had failed this test and been burned as a result.

His skin healed, though was far from the supple skin the selkie had possessed. His mother tended to the wounds daily, using ancient cures passed down from previous generations, but his eye was damaged beyond cure. The last thing it had seen was his father killing the selkie for him.

After his failure, his father had nothing to do with him, allowing him only little food and light. His mother filled his days teaching the young man ancient spells passed down from her grandmother.

He learned quickly, vowing never to fail again. It was seven long years in darkness before his father died and he was named Chief Rector of the Selkie Hunters.

Over the next several years he would grow to love the hunt, becoming a legend in their secret community. He cherished every murder, every drop of blood shed from the Unclean Ones.

So, on this night, he prayed to the old gods, thanking them for their help in finding the last known Selkie of the Americas. The half-breed would suffer for quite some time. This would be his punishment for his defiance. After the killing, he would enjoy his time with the girl, teaching her the ways of obedience and servitude to God and His servants. He enjoyed the thought of her becoming his special project. Yes, tonight was going to be very pleasant indeed.

Chapter Twenty-Three

As Aidan was dragged toward the bonfire, Deputy Paul Rheinstein was trying to talk Mary out of rushing the scene.

"We can't wait any longer!" Mary said.

"I agree. Please just wait here. If you see the other officers, let them know that I'm going in."

"Thank you, Paul."

He felt her hand on his elbow when he turned to leave. Rheinstein glanced back, studying the moonlight reflecting in her vibrant brown eyes.

"Promise you'll be careful," Mary said.

He flashed his disarming smile. "I promise."

Once the deputy disappeared beneath the cove, she said a silent prayer for his safety. Minutes later, she noticed several officers with flashlights making their way down the hillside. She waved her arms, trying to get their attention. Sheriff Carpenter was leading the group.

She pointed toward the bonfire. "Jade and Aidan are down there. Hurry! Deputy Rhenstein's on the scene. They're dragging Aidan to the fire and they have a knife!" Mary watched anxiously as the officers made their way down toward the shore.

JADE STRUGGLED DESPERATELY TO GET THE BODYGUARD TO RELEASE HER from his grip. His arms held her in a heavy vice, and she couldn't move. She watched helplessly while Aidan struggled against the rope tied to his neck. Thomas led him like an animal to slaughter.

"Stop it!" Jade screamed, as beastly moaning emanated from the sea. She turned toward the noise, watching in bewilderment at the pod of dark figures shadowing the tides. Slivers of moonlight illuminated dozens of elephant and harbor seals swimming to shore. Their eerie wails rose into a frenzied chorus.

Aidan could feel the heat of the fire when he was pushed closer to the flames. He looked up as the leader wielded a serrated knife above his ankles, ready to cut the meat from his bones.

"Pacific Grove Police Department! Drop your weapon or I'll shoot!" A loud voice wrung out from the distance and everyone turned. Deputy Paul stood on the overhang with gun in hand.

Ignoring the officer, the leader proceeded to bring the knife down.

The bullet whizzed by, cutting through the man's arm. He screamed in agony, stumbling toward the shore. The deputy yelled, "Stop or I'll shoot!"

The leader ignored the warning and headed toward the churning waves. Out of the dark waters emerged a massive pod of seals. The enormous beasts moved forth from the tides and immediately began galumphing onto the sandy shore. The leader of the Hunters tried to skirt away from the animals. He steadied his bleeding arm, dodging around two massive bulls. A second group cut him off on the right. A shrill scream erupted when a pair of harbor seals ploughed into him from the side, tearing through his right knee. The impact ripped open sinew and tendons, leaving him writhing on his back unable to move. He watched helplessly while the massive animals descended on him. His screams of terror mingled with the seals' barks and wails. Everyone watched in astonishment as the mammals piled onto the man, crushing his bones while ripping his flesh to pieces. When the marine mammals made their way back to the ocean, they left the bloody carcass in their path.

Jade screamed in horror at the sight of the carnage. With the death of their leader, the other Hunters scrambled over the beach, trying to make their way up the sandy hillside. Sheriff Carpenter and his officers immediately took chase. Thomas was halfway up the ice plant covered dune, nearly free, when Morrigan flew down from the cliff. The bird landed on his head and began pecking at his face. One of Sheriff Carpenter's deputies arrived while the raven tore gashes around the bodyguard's eyes and nose. After Thomas was in handcuffs, the rest of the men soon followed.

Finnean sat up weakly, blinking in confusion. An officer pulled him to his feet, handcuffing his arms behind his back. Mary, having climbed down from the ledge, ran over to Jade and helped her out of her restraints.

"Thank god you're safe," Mary said.

Jade smiled as the tears rolled down her cheeks. Morrigan flew from the hill, landing on her mistress' shoulder. She cawed, seeming quite pleased with herself.

"Oh, that's a good girl! I still have no idea how you escaped the cottage?"

Mary looked down at the ground. "I'm afraid she flew out the door when I let Dougal go outside to potty. I'm so sorry."

"Sorry?" Jade said. "You saved our lives! How on earth did you find us?"

Her friend smiled. "A dash of luck, a little help from Morrigan, some crazy dreams, and a bit of old-fashioned detective work," Mary said.

Aidan was helped to his feet by Deputy Rheinstein and released from his restraints. He patted the officer on his shoulder, smiling in gratitude. "Thank you, brother."

"No worries, buddy," Paul said.

When he was freed from the ropes, he rushed over, gathering Jade in his arms.

"Are you all right, love?" he said, holding her against him tightly.

"I'm fine. Are you hurt?" Jade asked.

"My feet are a bit sore, but I'll be fine. That fire was way too close for comfort."

Sheriff Carpenter gave orders to his men while they inspected the crime scene and brought the suspects back to the patrol units. Soon the beach was covered with yellow tape and detectives combing the scene. The coroner arrived not long after. Jade noticed one of the officers dragging Finnean up the hill.

"Wait, not the boy! He tried to help us escape. Their leader was planning to kill him. He wanted to get away from them. We said we would help him," she pleaded.

Sheriff Carpenter nodded "When we go back to the police station, you can brief us on everything, Miss Mackenzie."

The women glanced toward the beach. Bits of the Hunters' leader were strewn over the sand. Jade shuddered and looked away.

After all suspects were secured, Deputy Rheinstein drove Aidan, Mary, and Jade back to the police station. The women stayed late into the night answering questions and giving testimony. Once Sheriff Carpenter finished questioning the ladies, he requested Aidan and Paul stay behind for further debriefing. The deputy also needed to give a formal statement regarding the shooting.

Aidan took Jade's hands, kissing her on the forehead. "I promise I'll be back in the morning. The sheriff and I have quite a bit to discuss. I don't think this is quite over yet, but I'll be in touch once the questioning is over." He kissed her with gusto, leaving her gasping. "I'll make it up to you, I swear it, lass."

A red-headed deputy, George Finney, arrived soon after and drove the women and the pets back home. After they arrived at the cottage, they thanked the officer and hurried inside. Jade took a much-needed shower while Mary fed the animals and made a pot of hot cocoa.

Neither one was ready to go to bed, so they made a fire and curled beneath the blankets on the couch with their warm beverages. Dougal and Morrigan snuggled close while the women discussed their adventure.

It was closing in on three in the morning when Jade texted Aidan, letting him know they were still awake if there was any news. An hour later, there was a tap at the door. Aidan entered, to his dog's delight, along with Deputy Rheinstein.

"Hello, Paul," Mary said.

He took her hand, giving her a peck on the cheek.

"How did it go?" Jade asked.

"Well, the sheriff and I both had a feeling this wasn't over," Aidan said. "Finnean was interviewed along with the leader's henchman. He agreed to take a plea deal, no jail time, if he works with the Police Department with their investigation. Apparently, there's a large community of Selkie Hunters in Scotland. Sheriff Carpenter is planning on taking this to the FBI and Interpol. They'll keep him in protective custody until he's eighteen. Just another year or so."

Jade's eyes widened. "Would you mind if I had a word with you outside?" Aidan said.

"Absolutely." Jade looked back, noticing Mary preparing Paul a mug of cocoa. The officer grinned, admiring her culinary skills.

Aidan and Jade took a seat on the porch swing. "I have another proposition which I hope you'll consider."

"Oh?" Jade said.

"If there are selkie hunters active in Scotland, it's just a matter of time before they make it back to the States. I told you about my family castle in Tobermory."

"Yes." She searched his face in question.

"I want to investigate further. I was wondering if you might consider joining me overseas?"

"You're inviting me to Scotland to visit your castle and possibly hunt down Selkie Hunters?"

"Well, now that you put it that way, it seems a little overwhelming. I've been thinking about this on the drive over. I know you have your shop to consider. Is there any possibility of asking your friends to help while you're away?"

"I might be able to work something out for short period, but what about Morrigan and Dougal?" Jade asked.

He offered his lop-sided smile. "Don't worry about that, lass. We'll be flying private. It just so happens I own a jet."

Her eyes widened in disbelief.

"A private jet?"

He smiled, his blue eyes twinkling in the hazy light.

"I thought you weren't going to be keeping anymore secrets, Mr. MacFie?"

"It's not really a secret. It just never really came up." He chuckled, taking her hand in his.

"Well, I guess I could ask Mary to supervise part-time at my shop after I hire an assistant. Katie's in Ireland right now planning her wedding, so she's unavailable. I can make some calls to other friends around," Jade said, trying to hide her excitement.

He nodded. "So...it's a yes?" He gazed into her steel-gray eyes. "We make a pretty good team, lass."

"We do. Let me think this over for a moment," Jade said.

He stroked the side of her face with the back of his hand. She sighed at his gentle touch. Aidan held his breath awaiting her answer.

"I do believe a visit to the Highland Hills is way overdue. Let's go to Scotland!"

"Ah, lass. It will be an honor to be your guide." He swept up her into his arms, kissing her passionately beneath the Hunter's Moon.

She giggled and leaned into him.

He pulled her hips against his and held her tightly against him. Her breath hitched. "As soon as they leave, lass, I'll be keeping my promise to you."

She gasped as she felt heat begin to course through her body. "And what if they don't leave?" she managed.

His eyes burned into hers, making her glow and squirm. He grinned cheekily. "Then I'll have to bring you to my home to keep you safe. I'm sure they won't object to that."

As he lowered his mouth to hers, Jade desperately hoped that would be the case.

Chapter Twenty-Four

Jade sipped her flute of champagne, reclining comfortably against the velvet seat cushion and watched the pale mid-November sky fade away.

"A girl could get used to this luxury," she sighed. It had been five weeks since their rescue and they were on their way to Scotland to visit Aidan's family.

Aidan gave her a wink. "That's what I like to hear!"

"I'm glad. It's just disappointing that I wasn't able to talk to Topusana. I was so hoping to learn more about the Comanche. I guess I'll be investigating my Scottish side first," she said with a sigh. "Anyway, I heard from Mary before we boarded. She has coverage at The Muse Gallery for the next couple of weeks. She volunteered to work at the antique store until I get back. She seems pretty happy to be staying at the cottage while I'm gone," Jade said.

"Oh?"

"Yes, appears Deputy Rheinstein volunteered to continue checking in on her while we're gone. Those two have really seemed to hit it off. I'm happy for them."

Aidan smiled. "Paul's a standup guy. I'm glad they've taken a liking to each other."

"Me too. Oh, I almost forgot to tell you about the portrait. Mary told me the painting is back to normal. Can you believe it? The man is alone and on land again. It's like the changes never happened."

"Really?"

"Yep. It's a relief. The portrait was really starting to creep me out. Seeing the imagery change was like watching an episode of 'Night Gallery.' So spooky. I guess that's one mystery we didn't solve. I still have no idea where the painting came from."

"Well, at least it's gone back to normal for now. Hopefully, it will stay that way. Maybe we'll get some answers in Tobermory. My family is very excited to have us with them for the holidays."

She nodded. "I still can't believe we're leaving the country." She sighed. "I can't wait to see your ancestral home in Scotland. Are you going to change into a kilt when we arrive?"

He gave her a wink and his lopsided smile. "I'll do whatever my lass desires."

She giggled, imagining him in formal Scottish dress.

Aidan studied her face with adoring eyes. "You're a beauty, love."

He cupped her face, kissing her on the forehead. Afterward, he refreshed their glasses and placed the bottle back into the ice bucket. Once he handed her drink, he raised his glass.

"I'd like to make a toast."

She raised her glass in anticipation.

"To mysteries, adventures, and the great land of Scotland!"

They gazed into each other's eyes and clinked their crystal flutes. Aidan squeezed next to Jade on the lounge seat and took her hand in his. They both smiled, watching Morrigan and Dougal curled up across the aisle. Their pets had become inseparable in the last five weeks, choosing to bed down together even when their owners were not.

Aidan leaned down and whispered in her ear. "I love you, Miss Mackenzie."

"I love you, too, Mr. MacFie."

His lips found hers while the plane bounced in the turbulence. Lightning lit up the cabin compartment. Her breath hitched as his fingers slipped down her shoulders, grazing over her waist and hips. They lingered for a moment, before clicking the seatbelt over her lap. She gazed into his warm eyes while dimples rose in the corner of his cheeks.

"I'll always keep you safe, lass. Ye have my word."

She smiled up into his brilliant blue eyes.

"I know you will, love. You always have."

Aidan reached his arm around her shoulders while they braced for the impending storm. Jade leaned against his powerful body, realizing she'd finally found her place.

The End

Book 3 of the White Raven series
Selkies of Scotland
available Fall 2021

Don't miss out on your next favorite book!

Join the Satin Romance mailing list
www.satinromance.com/mail.html

About the Author

AnneMarie Dapp is a graduate of San Francisco State University, where she studied Studio Arts and Art History. She lives and writes on Sock Monkey Ranch, her and her husband Dale's vegan farm in Prunedale, California.

https://sockmonkey.live

facebook.com/AnneMarieDapp68

twitter.com/AnneMarieDapp

instagram.com/annemariedapp

pinterest.com/duckmomma1

Also by AnneMarie Dapp

White Raven Series

Prairie Ghosts

The Phantom Portrait

Selkies of Scotland *(coming Fall 2021)*

www.ingramcontent.com/pod-product-compliance
Lightning Source LLC
Chambersburg PA
CBHW020439180626
46812CB00003B/1312